The Last Cowboy

John Isaac Jones

For

Chiqui

Table of Contents

Reflections.. 1

Home On the Range... 5

In the Bunkhouse 11

The Crazy Horse 16

Easy Herd 21

Crazy Horse II... 28

Exodus.. 35

DeWayne 40

The Meeting... 48

Karina 57

Going to St. Louis.. 65

Friends 71

Ralph 78

Harold 82

Insurance Salesman 88

Crossing the Mississippi 94

The Commodore... 99

Memphis.. 106

Ghost 110

Nighttime at the Museum 118

DeWayne II.. 124

Selma 131

Drug Dealers... 140

Almost Home 148

Rancho Escobar 152

Romance.. 160

Jailbreak 166

Dogs, Bogs, and Logs 172

Dead End... 177

Wedding.. 183

Reflections II... 186

Reflections

It was late March of the year 2017 in Port Everglades, Florida. At the Rocking K Ranch outside of town, lifelong cowboy and ranch owner J.L Crockett, his hat and boots off, was relaxing in the front porch swing with an afternoon glass of sweetened iced tea. A sand and gravel lane, bordered on either side by a white wood slat fence, ran some one hundred yards from the ranch house to the main highway. Inside the fence on either side, a herd of white-faced cattle grazed quietly among scattered clumps of brush palmetto, cypress trees, and intermittent puddles of water left by a morning rain. High overhead, a flock of pelicans, flying in a broken V formation, glided silently. As J.L. swung quietly in the swing, he peered across the pasture. He was in an unusually reflective mood today.

You know, a man can do lots of things in this world, hoping it will bring him happiness, he thought. *He can make a lot of money, invent some new gadget, travel around the world, roll around with lots of women, or become world-famous in his chosen profession. Personally, I never had a lot of interest in any of those things. I always believed happiness was a level of satisfaction with yourself, a state of mind, so to speak. Something you feel inside your heart that confirms you are exactly at the point in your life you should be. In other words, you are perfectly in sync with your natural progression.*

I'm forty-four now and, thanks to Karina, I have finally found that happiness. When you're young, you have too many choices. There are too many things to do, too many places to go, and too many things to choose from. It takes some aging to realize what is important and meaningful in life.

Over the past ten years, I've been happier—no, more satisfied, more fulfilled—than I have ever been in my life. Karina has brought a fullness, a richness into my life that I could not have imagined before I met her. Every day, when I wake up, the first thing I do is turn to her and smile. I want to know what she's going to do today. I want to know how she's feeling, what she's thinking, her plans for today. My life is what it is today because of her. She is the center of my life, the core that binds all of the different parts of me into a single whole.

Now don't get me wrong. I loved my first wife. She was intelligent, good-hearted, hard-working, funny, and a good bedmate. Karina, on the other hand, has all of those qualities in spades. Of course, when I knew my first wife, I was a lot younger. Again, age makes so much difference in these things. As you age, your emotions tend to mature like fine wine. The joys and sorrows and laughter of youth become much deeper and richer in later years. At least they have for me. After my first wife passed, I thought I would never find another woman I could pour my heart into again. It's funny how karma takes care of those things.

My birth name is Jerome Lafayette Crockett. Where my mother came up with my first two names, I'll never know. I can tell you I never liked it, but it was Mama's choice, so I had to live with it, at least for the first few years. When I was nine, I asked my father and my friends to start calling me J.L. They agreed and it stuck. Since then, everybody just calls me J.L. It sounds a lot friendlier and is much easier to say than the names my mother gave me.

All I'd ever known in my life was cowboying. From the first day my daddy put me on a horse at age two in my native Oklahoma, all I ever loved was riding the open range, taking care of horses, roping cattle, and being around other cowboys. The smell of leather and horses and cattle are as much a part of my life as breathing and eating. All my life, I never felt comfortable wearing anything but my hat, a checkered shirt with pearl buttons, my boots, and jeans. I can put on a dress-up suit and a tie, but I always feel like I'm in a strait jacket.

His mind was quiet for a moment.

Now I hear Karina. I hear her footsteps coming down the hallway to the front porch.

"Baby?" a woman's voice called from inside.

"I'm out here," he said.

Karina Crockett, late thirties, smallish in stature, busty with pale skin and long jet-black hair, stepped out on the porch. She was wearing faded jeans and a blue checkered cowgirl shirt.

"What are you doing?" she asked.

"Relaxing," he said. "Is that okay?"

She smiled at him and offered her open right hand. His fingertips brushed across hers. She took a seat beside him on the swing and peered across the pasture.

"I thought you were going to move those white-face to the pasture across the road."

"No," J.L. said. "There is still plenty of grass in the front pasture. I'll have the boys move them tomorrow."

They sat quietly for several minutes, each lost in their own thoughts.

"It's almost three o'clock," she said finally, standing up. "I'm going to get the mail and meet Josh. I've got a roast in the oven. If I'm not back in fifteen minutes, go in there and turn it off. Okay?"

J.L. nodded.

He watched as she stepped off the porch and started walking along the lane to the main highway.

Every time I look at her, even after all these years, she always seems so incredibly sexy. Now as I watch her walk down the lane to the highway, I imagine her being naked. She's fully clothed, but when I see those hips swinging back and forth in those tight jeans, I see bare flesh in my mind. As she walks, her breasts jostle slightly underneath the blue-checkered shirt, but all I see are wonderfully formed mounds of womanly flesh in sync with her every step. Lots of times, when I see her like this, I want to run to her, tear her clothes off, and throw her on the ground and make love to her, but I couldn't really do something like that. It's just a fantasy. I have too much love and respect for her to do something like that.

I guess you could say I've been lucky. I've known lots of men who never found the right woman in their life. I've also known men who spent their entire lives with a woman they didn't really like. After a couple kids and a mortgage, they were locked in and just toughed it out. I never was much of a religious person, but I've always been a firm believer in karma. If you do good things in this world, good things will come back to you. If you harm or abuse other people, I believe you can expect bad things to come into your life. I've always tried to be a good person and I believe that's the reason Karina is part of my life today. Even now, I'm not exactly sure why karma saw fit to bring us together, but I'm eternally thankful it happened.

I might as well tell you now you're not going to believe the story you're about to hear. You're probably going to think I'm crazy, but most of my life seems to have been governed by chance, happenstance, and just plain old coincidence. I'm talking about crazy things that suddenly pop up for no rhyme or reason and brings huge changes to your life. That's what this story is about. Like I said, some of these things are unbelievable, but I swear every word you're about to hear is true.

Okay, I won't keep you waiting any longer. The story you are about to hear happened ten years ago. It covers a span of about two weeks in my life; a span that changed my life forever. This is the story of me and Karina. It's a tale that relates how we met, fell in love, got married, and arrived at the life we have today. This is our story.

Home On the Range

March, 2007

In eastern Washington State, just south of Spokane, the mighty Cascade Range slopes erratically downward to a low, expansive plateau known as the Columbia River Basin. Over a period of 10 to 15 million years, this massive earthen bowl was formed between the Cascades and the Rockies when millions of tons of molten lava from local volcanoes engulfed an estimated 63,000 square miles of the earth's surface. As the lava cooled, the earth's crust slowly but surely pushed itself into the cracks and crevices left by the rising lava and brought with it billions upon billions of tons of rich, fertile topsoil, which proved ideal for humankind to grow alfalfa hay, wheat, apples, and beef cattle. As a result, by the early 20th century, numerous farms and cattle ranches had sprung up across the plateau to take advantage of these fertile conditions. It was here on one of these ranches, a sprawling 10,000-acre spread called the Lazy B, that thirty-four-year-old J.L. found himself one afternoon in the early spring of 2007.

On this particular day, J.L. and another cowboy, Carl "Curly" Watson, were riding fence through one of the ranch's lush river valleys. With J.L. on an Appaloosa stallion and Curly on a smaller paint, they followed an aspen-studded trail along a fence line that stretched endlessly to the horizon.

"Sometimes, I don't know what to make of her," Curly was saying as the horses ambled slowly along the fence trail. "I love her, but she sure is bossy. Whenever I'm around her, it's always 'do this, do that.'"

J.L looked thoughtfully over at his friend.

"And she wants everything she sees," Curly continued, shaking his head in indecision. "She wants silly things she doesn't really need. She just thinks she wants them."

Curly smiled his trademark boyish grin. Although he was twenty-four, he could easily pass for eighteen or nineteen. Medium height, clean-cut, always smiling, Curly looked up to J.L. and was forever seeking his fatherly advice. His name was Carl, but with a headful of curly brown hair, the nickname Curly had stuck during the four years he'd been at the Lazy B.

"If you love her, I mean, really love her, all of that won't matter in the long run," J.L. replied.

"Yeah, maybe you're right," Curly said with a sigh. "I guess I just don't understand women."

They rode quietly.

"Women are like anything in life," J.L. said philosophically. "You only get out of them what you put into them. It's basic karma."

"I never thought of it that way," Curly said thoughtfully.

J.L. didn't reply at first.

"Me, I'll never get married again," J.L. said finally. "Once was enough. I don't think I could ever find another woman I loved as much as Sara."

"Yeah, I know she meant a lot to you," Curly said.

"I always wanted a son with her, but nature just didn't want to cooperate," J.L. continued with a deep sigh. "I guess that's just the way it is sometimes. Nothing on this earth would've made me happier than having a son. I'd watch him grow up and teach him to rope and to ride and cut cattle—but I guess it'll never be."

The two rode silently. The aspen grove along the fence trail had thinned out and the scenery had become a grassy, rolling meadow carpeted with billions of sagebrush violets. The two horses plodded lazily across the short grass in the meadow, their hooves softly brushing aside the purple flowers.

"Ever talk to your brother Harold?" J.L. asked.

"He called about six months ago," Curly replied. "He always asks about you. He still remembers the time you and him got drunk down at the Crazy Horse."

J.L. laughed happily. "Yeah, that brother of yours is about as crazy as I am. What's he doing these days?"

"He's back in St. Louis," Curly replied. "He wanders all over, but he always ends up back in St. Louis."

Curly and his older brother Harold had grown up in St. Louis. J.L. had heard lots of stories about their childhood years.

"I never been to St. Louis," J.L. said after a long pause. "I always wanted to walk under that big arch they have over the Mississippi River."

"Yeah, it's something to see."

"One of these days, I'm going to take a trip across these United States and see all the things I always wanted to see. The St. Louis Arch, Mount Rushmore, Little Big Horn, and that place Elvis built for his mother in Memphis. And I'd love to see that Civil War display they got in Atlanta. And the swamps in Florida and South Georgia. You know, there's a lot of history in this country."

Curly nodded in agreement.

The two cowboys rode quietly for several minutes. Ahead of them, along the trail, J.L. saw a small trout stream winding across the meadow.

"Let's stop up here and get some water," he said.

Moments later, they dismounted at the trout stream. J.L. took a canteen from his saddlebag and approached the stream. As he strode through the short grass to the water's edge, he struck a portrait of the classic American Cowboy. Tall with wide, muscular shoulders, narrow waist, and a tight, weather-beaten face, his rugged, ready appearance testified to many years of riding the range.

Suddenly, J.L. stopped and pointed into the clear, crystal water.

"Look at that speckled trout," he said.

Curly peered into the stream.

"Yep," Curly replied. "He'll go two pounds, easy."

J.L. removed his black hat and got down on his knees to

7

drink from the snow-fed stream. He took several swigs of cool, clear water, then filled his canteen and stood up.

"Look up there, Curly," J.L. said happily, raising his face full to the endless blue sky above. "That sky just goes on and on and on and on."

Curly looked up.

"I don't see nothing," he said, peering up at the sky disinterestedly. "It looks like it's always looked to me."

"That's forever," J.L. continued happily. "That sky represents eternity. All of that was here before us, and it will be here after we're gone."

"If you say so, J.L.," Curly replied.

"There is no life greater than the life of a cowboy," J.L. continued, peering across the meadow at the ranch and the snow-capped mountains beyond. "Being out in the open with the wind and the rain and the wide open spaces. Money can't make me happy. Only the stars, the open skies, and the open range make me happy. Fresh air, clean water, and green everywhere you look. What more could a man ask for? Think of all the poor guys that have to put on a zoot suit and go into an office every day. I'll tell you, Curly, I wouldn't give up my life as a cowboy for nothing on this earth."

J.L. peered across the meadow toward the ranch in the valley below.

"Look," he said, pointing toward the ranch. "Carlos and Sonny are going in."

Curly peered toward the ranch in the distance.

"Come on," J.L. said. "I'll race you to the corral."

J.L. quickly turned from the stream and sprang into the saddle.

"Let's go, Rebel!" he barked to the stallion.

The mighty horse lifted its head and in a single leap launched into a full gallop. Not to be outdone, Curly swung up into the saddle of the paint, spurred its side, and seconds later was in a full gallop behind the Appaloosa.

It was a majestic sight, those two. Two American cowboys on muscular horses, streaking across an endless purple meadow against a backdrop of snow-covered mountains. It was the American spirit rolled into a single image. A portrait of pure Americana. The embodiment of the American soul.

While the stallion had longer legs and could take longer strides, the paint's shorter legs could move faster, and at one hundred yards into the race, the paint pulled up neck in neck to the larger horse. The stallion, however, at the moment he felt the smaller horse was pulling up to him, sensed the challenge, and with one mighty burst of energy, raced ahead of the paint to the corral.

At the corral, J.L. reined in the stallion and dismounted. Seconds later, Curly was right behind him. J.L. opened the gate and the two cowboys led their horses into the corral and headed toward the barn. In one corner of the corral, they saw Sonny, a blonde, baby-faced, nineteen-year-old and the ranch's youngest cowboy, brushing down a roan. Nearby, Carlos, a stocky Latin man, was brushing down another horse.

For a moment, J.L. stopped and studied the younger cowboy.

"Sonny," J.L. said, walking over and taking charge. "Brush him down top to bottom."

J.L. took the brush and moved it across the horse with expert even strokes.

"See what I mean?" J.L. said.

"Yeah," Sonny said agreeably.

"He is young," Carlos said in a heavy Spanish accent. "He has much to learn."

J.L. laughed, turned, and started into the barn with the stallion.

As J.L. and Curly led their horses into the barn, Will Hansen—the tall, sunburned, early fiftyish ranch foreman—was coming out of the barn.

"How's that fence over at Teakettle Mountain?" the foreman asked.

"The spring rains washed out some of the rocks, but we shored it up."

"Can a calf get under it?" Will asked.

9

"Oh no," J.L. said. "We stacked those rocks up to the bottom strand of barbed wire."

"Good," Will replied.

J.L. glanced into one of the stalls. Inside, he saw a man in a white jacket tending to a steer. The man was seated on a blacksmith's stool, fitting some sort of metal device into the steer's hoof.

"Hey, mister," he said. "What are you doing to that steer?"

The man in the white coat looked up at J.L., obviously annoyed.

J.L. moved closer. "What's that piece of metal you're putting in that cow's hoof?"

Another man, wearing a Hawaiian shirt and several gold chains and looking starkly out-of-place for a working ranch, appeared.

"Hey, cowboy," he said to J.L, "what do you want?"

"What's he doing to that cow?"

The man in the polo shirt turned.

"Foreman!" he yelled.

Will stepped over and surveyed the scene. He turned to J.L. "They don't want you here," Will said firmly.

"What's he doing?" J.L. asked for the fourth time.

"This is some of Frank Junior's stuff," the foreman said. "I'll tell you guys about this later. Just put your horse up and go on into the bunkhouse."

In the Bunkhouse

The bunkhouse at the Lazy B was an aging, two-story, wood-frame structure with sleeping quarters on the upper level and living quarters, an after-hours kitchen, and a laundry room on the bottom floor. It sat snugly behind the main ranch house within easy walking distance to the ranch kitchen, corral, and barns. Inside the main living area, the Western, wood-heavy décor testified to many years of habitation by a long line of professional cowboys. At one end of the main room, there was a giant, ceiling-high fireplace with an array of cowboy heroes smiling down. Directly over the fireplace mantel, an autographed photo of Roy Rogers served as centerpiece. Supplementing Rogers were photos of William S. Hart, Bob Steele, John Wayne, Tex Ritter, Gene Autry, Gary Cooper, Alan Ladd, and Clint Eastwood. Also on the mantel, there was an extensive collection of photos of former Lazy B cowboys and an assortment of other ranch memorabilia. In a sitting area in front of the fireplace, all of the ranch cowboys, having had their showers, were relaxing after a hard day on the range.

On the sofa, J.L. and Curly were glued to a television, watching the Humphrey Bogart-Katherine Hepburn classic, *The African Queen*. Carlos and Sonny were seated nearby, playing checkers. Sonny was intently studying his next move as Carlos watched. Finally, Sonny picked up a checker and made a jump.

"Wait a minute," Carlos said defiantly. "You can't move backwards."

"You can if it's a king," Sonny shot back defensively.

"Oh, these American games!" Carlos protested. "They never make any sense."

Carlos looked over at J.L. who, along with Curly, couldn't take his eyes off the television. They were watching the scene in the movie where Bogart and Hepburn were captured by the Germans and told by the fat, baby-faced ship's captain that they were going to be hung as spies.

"J.L.!" Carlos called.

Instantly, J.L. put his fingers to his lips, indicating that he couldn't be disturbed.

"I got a question," Carlos pressed.

"Shhhh, not now," J.L. said again more emphatically.

Carlos, looking very frustrated, returned to the checkers.

Onscreen, Bogart turned to the ship's captain and said, "You're a ship's captain; you can marry people, can't you?"

"Oh, Charlie," the Hepburn character replied happily.

"God, I love that scene," J.L. said blissfully. "It's one of my favorite scenes from a movie."

As J.L. turned back to Carlos to answer his question, Will stepped into the bunkhouse's living quarters and everyone's attention turned to the boss.

"Frank Jr. has called a meeting for tomorrow morning at seven a.m.," he said. "It's going to be big, so everybody has to be there."

"Has it got anything to do with the guy in the white jacket I saw in the barn today?" J.L. asked.

"I can't say anything," Will replied, shaking his head. "Just make sure all you guys are there tomorrow."

All the cowboys nodded their approval and Will stepped out.

The Bogart-Hepburn movie had ended, so J.L., remote in hand, started flipping through the channels. He stopped on a local news program.

The announcer was stating, "Police said the founder and chief executive of a major software manufacturing company in Renton was found dead in his home today, apparently the victim of a self-inflicted gunshot wound. A suicide note stated that the victim was tired of making money—"

J.L. flipped the channel again. He flipped past a cooking

show, a baseball game, and finally stopped on a religious program.

The minister, holding a Bible in one hand and gesturing with the other, was saying, "And Jesus said, 'Let not your heart be troubled. Ye believe in God, believe also in me—'"

Disinterestedly, J.L. flipped through several more channels and then threw the remote on the couch.

"There's nothing on," he said. "I'm going to the Crazy Horse."

"Make that two," Curly said.

"Make that three," Sonny added.

"What about the checkers game?" Carlos asked, still sitting at the table and waiting for Sonny to return. "When I'm about to win, you want to leave."

"You can't win," Sonny said.

"What do you mean?" Carlos said.

Sonny walked over to the table.

He picked up his king and jumped the last four of Carlos's pieces.

"That's why!"

Carlos grimaced in defeat.

"These crazy American games," he said, getting up from the table. "Come on; let's go to the Crazy Horse."

Twenty minutes later, J.L. and Curly were in J.L.'s pickup, cruising down Highway 63 toward town.

"Can we stop at the Quick Shop?" Curly asked. "I need to get some shaving gear and a copy of *American Cowboy*."

"That's fine," J.L. said. "I've got to stop for gas."

Ten minutes later, J.L. pulled the pickup off the main highway and stopped in front of the pump.

"Anything I can get you?" Curly asked as he got out.

"I'll be in there in a minute," J.L. said, lifting the nozzle to pump the gas.

Ten minutes later, J.L. emerged from the station office and returned to the pickup. Curly was already inside, swilling a beer and thumbing through a magazine. As J.L. slid into the driver's seat, he carefully placed two fresh red roses and a twelve-pack of Fancy Fruit chewing gum on the seat between them. J.L. opened the carton of chewing gum, took out a pack, and then started the engine.

Curly looked down at the roses. "You still holding on?" he asked. "It's been two years."

"She's all I ever had," J.L. replied.

Curly, knowing better than to pursue the subject further, turned back to the magazine. J.L. opened the package of chewing gum, unwrapped a stick, and popped it in his mouth.

"Want a piece?" J.L. asked.

"Not with this beer," Curley replied.

J.L. wadded up the chewing gum wrapper and tossed it at the open ashtray. The wadded wrapper hit the ashtray's edge, bounced off, and hit the truck floor.

"You missed," Curly observed playfully.

"The sweeper will get it tomorrow," J.L. replied, and both men laughed.

* * *

Ten minutes later, J.L. maneuvered the pickup off the main highway onto a narrow, gravel road and up a hill. As he negotiated the truck up the winding road, they passed a sign that proclaimed "Elk Mountain Baptist Church." Moments later, they passed a small, one-room white church with a bell tower, a steeple, and a white cross on top. Finally, J.L. brought the truck to a stop beside a small country cemetery.

"I'll be back in a minute," he said, taking the roses and getting out.

"Take your time," Curly said, his face buried in the magazine.

Roses in hand, J.L. strode gingerly through the rows of graves and finally stopped in front of a headstone that read "Sara Jane Crockett 1975–2005."

For a moment, he stared sadly at the headstone. He bent down and pulled some new weeds that obscured the name. With his boot, he leveled the dirt surface of the grave to make it more uniform. Then he removed two wilted roses from a glass vase atop the grave and replaced them with the fresh

14

ones. Finally, satisfied that the grave was presentable again, he took off his hat and stood silently.

"I think about you every day," he said finally. "It's springtime now. The spring run-off is feeding all the flowers and the yellow honeysuckle is in bloom. Every time I smell honeysuckle, I remember me and you walking down the lane at your parents' house in Cheyenne. You were wearing that blue, flowery dress and I was holding your hand, and you were laughing at my silly jokes. I was so happy. Nobody else ever laughed at my stupid jokes, but you did. Nothing made me happier than seeing you laughing and brushing your hair back and smiling at me. That's all I ever wanted—just to be close to you."

For a moment, he stopped and looked away. Then, he repositioned the glass vase, pulled some more weeds, and did a final inspection on the grave. Finally, he brushed away tears, put his hat back on, and headed back to the pickup.

The Crazy Horse

The Crazy Horse Saloon was the regular watering hole for the local cowboys. Housed in a wooden, tin-roofed, barn-looking structure, it sat alone on the side of the highway. Perched high atop the building was a poorly painted sign depicting the legendary Sioux Chief—Crazy Horse.

Inside, the saloon was a din of clinking beer glasses, clicking pool balls, heavy smoke, and the smell of stale beer. The Lazy B cowboys were seated at a corner table.

The moment J.L. and Curly entered the door, Harvey the bartender looked up from the drink he was pouring and saw them.

"J.L.!" he called.

J.L. smiled and waved. Harvey was a long-time friend was always trying to fix him up with some woman. Moments later, after serving the drink, Harvey ducked out from behind the bar and approached them

"Good to see you, J.L.," Harvey said, offering his hand. "Come on over here. I got somebody I want you to meet."

Uh, oh, J.L. thought, *here we go again.*

Harvey escorted J.L. over to the end of the bar where he saw what local cowboys referred to as a dinette—a female tourist from the city who wanted to rub elbows with real cowboys. She was a tall, well-tanned brunette in her late thirties and decked out in newly outfitted jeans, a cowgirl hat, and boots.

"This is my cousin, Lauren, all the way from Los Angeles, California," Harvey said. "She's staying at a dude ranch over at Carlson."

Lauren looked up from her drink, examined J.L., and

offered her hand. "Hello," she said politely.

"Pleasure to meet you," J.L. said equally politely, taking her hand.

"Do you play pool?" she asked.

"Sure," J.L. said, glancing over at the bar's two pool tables and seeing that the one nearest the Lazy B crew was free.

"Let's play over there," he said. "I can talk to my friends while we play. Get the table and I'll get some beers."

* * *

Ten minutes later, J.L. and the brunette were playing eight ball. J.L. was sipping beer and watching her shoot. At the nearby table, Curly was reading his *American Cowboy* magazine.

"Hey, J.L." Curly said, looking up from the magazine. "Look at these boots."

Curly got up, walked over to J.L., and pointed out an advertisement in the magazine. J.L. peered at the ad.

"Double-stitched uppers. Leather soles with foam rubber inlays," Curly said. "Now that's a nice pair of boots."

J.L. took the magazine. "Yeah," J.L. said, peering at the ad. "Kind of expensive, but nice."

Then his eyes moved from the boot ad and stopped at another part of the page.

"Hey, what's this?" he asked, peering at the advertisement. "American Cowboys!" he read aloud. "Ride the Range with the Gauchos!"

J.L. glanced up from the magazine and turned to the table where the other Lazy B cowboys were seated. "Hey, guys! Listen to this!"

The other cowboys turned their attention to J.L.

"Welcome, American Cowboys," J.L. read aloud from the magazine. "Rancho Palermo wants YOU! Rancho Palermo, the largest cattle ranch in Argentina, is seeking American cowboys who want to spend the rest of their lives on the range. Perfect candidate will be in his early forties, have at least fifteen years of experience, including herding, branding, roping, and horsemanship—"

17

"Hey, cowboy," Lauren interrupted. "It's your shot."

"Hang on," J.L. said. "I'm not finished. 'At Rancho Palermo, we want cowboys who can work cattle on the range until age sixty and then retire to our dude ranch near Casa Grande, Argentina, and teach young kids from America, Europe, and Asia how to ride a horse. Free passage from Miami to Buenos Aires via luxury ship *La Señora*. Competitive wages. All successful applicants must bring own guitar. To apply, please call 1-800-783-0021.'"

Curly smirked. "It's a rip-off," he said. "They'll get you on that boat, take your money, and dump you in the ocean. You'll never see a ranch. Or a horse."

Will laughed. "They don't use ropes down there to handle cattle," he said. "They use balls on leather strings."

"They're called bolas," J.L. said, still peering at the advertisement. "Sounds pretty interesting to me." He handed the magazine back to Curly.

"Your shot, cowboy," Lauren said impatiently. "You've got an easy shot on the eight."

J.L crouched down over the cue ball and made the eight to win the game.

"Good shot," she said. "Come on; let's take our beers and go out back where it's quiet."

"We can do that," he said.

***

Five minutes later, J.L. and Lauren were sitting in the deserted dining area at the rear of the saloon. The night was quiet and, somewhere in the distance, they could hear the lonesome wail of a coyote

"Tell me about yourself," she started.

"There's not a lot to tell," he said. "Grew up on my father's ranch in Oklahoma, was a fair halfback in high school, and made average grades. After high school, my father sent me to the University of Oklahoma. I thought college was the stupidest thing I'd ever seen."

"Stupid?"

"They put me in a class where it takes them four months to

teach me the contents of one book. I could sit down and read the book and know most everything in it in a couple of days."

"So what happened?" she asked, sipping her beer.

"I stopped going to class and started going to the library and read books all day."

"What did you read?" she asked.

"Everything that matters—Plato, Aristotle, Freud, Darwin, Nietzsche, Marx, Kant, Schiller, Montaigne, and lots of poetry. Especially the romantics."

"I'm impressed," she said thoughtfully. "So you've traveled in the realms of gold."

He smiled. "Yes," he said. "And many goodly states and kingdoms seen," he added, finishing the line from the Keats poem.

She laughed. "In Xanadu did Kubla Khan a stately pleasure dome decree..." she quoted.

"Where Alph, the sacred river, ran through caverns measureless to man, down to a sunless sea," J.L replied. "I'm very familiar with the works of Coleridge."

"My! My!" she said. "I'm impressed. What does the 'J.L.' stand for?"

"That's a long story," he said.

"You mean you don't want to talk about it?"

He grinned.

"So what did you do after college?" she asked.

"I realized that all I ever wanted to do was to be a cowboy and roam the world. The world is too big and too varied and too wonderful to spend all your life in one place. I was a professional bronco rider in the rodeo for a few years. I toured for a while. Got a few bones broke. Even after I was married, I continued to wander—"

"Married?"

"Well, not anymore," he said. "She passed away two years ago."

"Sorry to hear that," she said apologetically.

There was a long pause.

In the distance, they heard the plaintive wail of the coyote again.

"Tell me about your life," he said.

She took another swig of beer and inhaled deeply. "I'm this poor little rich girl from Santa Monica who roams the world collecting men," she said wistfully. "When I was growing up, my father owned six banks and all I ever had to do was go to school and look pretty for him. I have a bachelor's from UCLA, a master's from Berkeley, and a Ph.D. from Harvard in English Literature."

"You mean I can call you 'doctor'?"

"You can, but I'd prefer you didn't," she said.

"You say you collect men?"

"Men are the most fascinating creatures on earth."

"That's a broad statement," he said and laughed. "But I have to say that I agree."

There was another long pause.

"You're not only smart, you're good-looking," she said. "Did you know that?"

"Thank you," he replied. "You're not unattractive yourself."

She smiled.

"Are you going to add me to your collection?" J.L. asked.

"The night's not over," she said with a sly grin.

He laughed. At the back door, Curly appeared.

"We're going in," Curly said. "Want me to ride back to the ranch with Will?"

"No, that's okay," J.L. said. "I've got to be going too."

He got up and offered his hand. "Lauren, I enjoyed talking to you and playing pool."

She took his hand and held it tightly.

"So did I," she said. "Are you sure you can't stay and have a few more beers? I can take you back to the ranch."

"No, I need to get in," he said. "We've got a big meeting with the ranch owner tomorrow. I need to be there bright and early."

"Okay," she said. "I'll walk out with you."

Easy Herd

The following morning, all of the Lazy B cowboys and their foremen were gathered in the south pasture. In front of them stood ranch owner Frank Bradford Jr., a short, stocky man in his early forties. Behind him stood a tallish, well-tanned man in a Hawaiian shirt, wearing sunglasses and a cowboy hat. This was the man who had called the foreman on J.L. the previous day in the corral. Off to the side, the cowboys could see a cattle transport truck with a bull, two cows, and several calves inside. Beside the truck sat an open-air Jeep with a small satellite dish on the hood. Inside sat another man wearing a Hawaiian shirt, with a laptop computer mounted on the console. The men in the Hawaiian shirts stood in sharp contrast to the natural surroundings and the unpretentious cowboys.

The ranch owner stepped forward and motioned for quiet. "Morning, boys," he said. For a moment, he stood silently as he surveyed the assemblage. Finally, he took a deep breath and exhaled.

"It's a sad day," he said finally. "For me, for you, and for all cowboys." He stopped again. "I've known some of you men all my life," he continued wistfully. He looked at Will. "I was eight years old when you went to work for my daddy," he reminisced. "You taught me to use a curry comb and tie a martingale on a horse. I'll always remember the time my horse lost a shoe over at Box Canyon and we rode double back to the ranch."

He stopped again and looked at Curly. "How long you been at the Lazy B?" he asked.

"Since I was nineteen," Curly said. "Same age as Sonny."

The ranch owner glanced at J.L.

"Eight years," J.L. replied.

The ranch owner looked downcast for a moment, took another deep breath, and then turned back to the cowboys.

"When I got my degree in ranch management over in Laramie, I knew technology was going to change ranching forever; it was just a matter of time. I didn't know when, but I knew it was coming. Like everything else in this modern world, computers are taking over every part of our lives. The way we work, the way we think, the way we play, the way we pay our bills—the way we do everything. Now computers are replacing cowboys."

"What?" Will blurted out in disbelief.

"It's true," the ranch owner replied sadly. "Computers, along with satellites, can now herd and brand cattle without horses, saddles, ropes, and cowboys."

The cowboys looked at one another in disbelief.

"No!" Will said again.

"I'm afraid so," the ranch owner repeated. "Let me introduce you men to Lance Worthington," he said, indicating the man beside him in the cowboy hat and Hawaiian shirt. Lance is president of Western Liquidators, a computer programming company in San Francisco. He'll tell you all about it."

The man in the Hawaiian shirt stepped forward. "Good morning, everyone," he began. "As all of you know, the world is changing rapidly," he said. "Technology is changing people at a rate faster than they can absorb the changes. For many years, cowboys have ridden horses to round up cattle and drive them into corrals and herding stalls. Now all of that is changing. Let me introduce my friend Bobby Woolford, the cowboy of the future," he said, waving his hand to present the man in the Jeep with the laptop. "Me and Bobby have been working together for a long time."

The man in the Jeep raised his fist triumphantly at the introduction. The assembled cowboys did not applaud.

"Bobby," Lance ordered, motioning toward the cattle

transport truck, "go ahead and unload the test herd. Put those animals right here in front of us."

Lance stepped forward and drew an X in the dirt with the toe of his cowboy boot.

His assistant punched some keys on the laptop.

The gate to the cattle transport truck magically opened. An unloading platform slid out from under the bed of the truck for the cattle to walk on. All six animals—three calves, two cows, and Roscoe, the ranch's prize bull—walked unsteadily down the unloading platform and then trotted over to the precise spot the presenter had indicated.

The Lazy B cowboys watched with amazement.

"How'd you do that?" Will asked.

With that, the presenter held up a shiny silver computer disk.

"This is Easy-Herd," he said, "the computer program that replaces cowboys."

"That's crazy!" Curly yelled.

"I've never heard of such," said J.L.

"Fellows! Fellows!" the presenter said, trying to bring order. "Let me finish."

Once order was restored, the presenter continued.

"With this program, a ranch owner can sort a herd of cattle any way he wants. He can put calves and bulls in one corral and stallions and mares in another. It has been thoroughly tested with sheep in Australia and horses in Montana. But, obviously, the most useful purpose is for cattle. That's why we're here today."

The presenter stepped forward and approached the bull. Using a pointer, he motioned to the animal's hooves.

"Electromagnetic sensors have been placed on either side of this animal's hooves. These detectors are in direct contact with its central nervous system and the muscles in its legs. When a signal is sent from this dish," he said, indicating the receiver mounted on the hood of the Jeep, "to a satellite 21,000 miles out in space, Bobby can send electronic impulses to those detectors, and the animal will move accordingly. If the animal moves in the wrong direction, the chip emanates a mild electrical shock to the required portion of the animal's brain. If the animal moves in the desired direction, a warm, glowing, peaceful sensation emanates from the chip. We recommend that the computer chips be embedded in a young calf at around fifteen days old. Young animals will respond to the chip's commands immediately. Once the chips are implanted, that animal is at the mercy of the person operating the computer. This means a ranch owner can move all of his animals from one designated pasture to another with the push of a button."

The Lazy B cowboys were mesmerized by what they were seeing and hearing.

"Depending on the size of the herd, Easy-Herd will solve the most difficult of herding tasks," Lance continued. "Studies have shown that no matter the task, whether branding, herding, or cutting cattle, Easy-Herd can perform chores 1,422 times faster than the traditional cowboy on a horse."

The Lazy B cowboys were in silent awe.

"Of course," the presenter continued, "pasture locations are based on latitude and longitude and must be programmed into the software. Let me demonstrate."

He turned to his assistant.

"Bobby," he said, "make that red calf run out into the pasture for about a hundred yards."

The assistant punched a key on the laptop.

The cowboys watched as the young calf's entire body suddenly trembled. Then, from a dead stop, the animal lurched forward into a full run into the pasture and then quickly stopped.

"My God!" Will shouted. "Do you have any idea what you're doing to that poor animal?"

"That's technology," Lance said.

"Do you give a damn what you're doing to that calf?" Will asked.

Lance looked at him with hard eyes and said nothing.

Will shook his head in disbelief.

"All right, Bobby, bring that red calf back over here."

The assistant punched some more keys and the calf, panting heavily, broke into a full run and then came to a screeching halt in front of the assemblage. The assistant was giggling with glee.

"Obviously, the bigger the animal, the more voltage is required to move them," Lance continued. "Bobby, put that cow into a Cheyenne two-step."

With that, the assistant punched some keys on the laptop.

All the cowboys watched in amazement as the cow trembled momentarily, moved sideways two steps, and then took two steps in the opposite direction.

"You've heard of the Cincinnati dancing pig?" the presenter said gleefully. "Here you have the Spokane dancing cow."

The man with the laptop laughed out loud.

"We haven't actually choreographed it to music yet, but there are lots of things you can do because you have complete control over the animal and its movements."

Lance stopped for a moment and surveyed the cowboys.

"Now I'm sure all you men have seen a bull get aggressive at times," the presenter said. "You get off your horse, you're minding your own business, and then suddenly, a bull that you thought was perfectly peaceful is charging at you."

He looked at Will.

"Have you ever had an angry bull charge you?" he asked.

"Yeah, yeah," Will said impatiently.

"Let me show you what Easy-Herd can do," the presenter said, taking a wadded-up red handkerchief out of his back pocket.

"What are you doing?" Will asked. "Are you crazy?"

"Shhhh!" the presenter said, putting his finger to his lips, indicating for Will to remain calm.

He turned to his assistant.

"Okay, Bobby," he said. "When I tell you, hit control-V on the keyboard."

With that, he unfurled the red handkerchief and waved it in

front of the bull. The bull's lower lip instantly curled in anger and then it went into a forward crouching position and started pawing the ground.

"Hit Control-V," Lance said to his cohort.

The associate punched some keys on the laptop.

Suddenly, the angry bull lurched forward in a full charge toward the presenter.

"Yaaaaaaiiii!" the presenter screamed in fear as he saw the angry animal charging at him. He broke into a full run to escape.

Then, as the assemblage watched, the bull chased the presenter out into the pasture. After running about one hundred yards out, the presenter turned and started running full speed back toward the assemblage, the angry bull right on his heels. Lance was running for dear life.

As the presenter and the angry bull neared the assemblage, Lance, who was scared out of his wits, yelled at his associate. "Control-V! Control-V!" he screamed at the top of his lungs.

"C for Charley?" the associate yelled back.

"V for Victor!" the presenter screamed.

The computer operator carefully studied the keyboard, then hit the correct combination of keys. Suddenly, the raging bull stopped dead in its tracks, looked at the assemblage, then started quietly grazing. The bull was now as calm as a newborn calf. Seeing the animal was contained, a big smile of relief flashed across Lance's face and he walked back to the presenter's space in front of the crowd.

"There," he said, finally regaining his breath. "Now you have seen what Easy Herd can do to a raging bull."

Over the next twenty minutes, he explained how the new virtual cowboy could control every part of a herd. He showed them how it could open and close gates and how microchips could be implanted into an animal's ear to locate and identify it no matter where it had been lost. He explained how it could also be used to automatically feed a herd in the pasture or in the barn. Finally, after the demonstration was completed, the ranch owner stepped forward.

"Well, fellows, I guess you all know what this means. Lance here says he'll need about two days to finish up the implants. That means, as of the day after tomorrow, Friday, April 14, I'll no longer be in need of your cowboying services. I want to thank all you men for the work you've put into making the Lazy B a successful ranching operation. Will will settle up with each of you on Friday. I promise I'll be generous to each of you in your termination package. Again, I want to say thanks. Anybody got anything to say?"

"Frank Jr.," Will said. "If your father knew what was happening here today, he'd roll over in his grave."

The ranch owner looked at his foreman. "You're probably right, Will," he said seriously. "But times change. My father was old school. He was a 20th century rancher. This is the 21st century now. In the new century, cowboying will be done with computers."

"You can't just do away with a whole profession because of a new machine," Will said.

"You're wrong, Will," the ranch owner said. "We can. And we're doing it. I'm sorry, men."

With that, the ranch owner cast his head downward, turned quickly, and walked to his truck without looking back. As the Lazy B cowboys watched, he got into the truck and drove away.

Crazy Horse II

Back at the Crazy Horse that night, the soon-to-be-jobless Lazy B cowboys were getting tears in their beers.

"It's an abomination," Will, who was already drunk, said to the other cowboys. "What would this country be without cowboys? The world is forgetting that the very fabric of the American spirit is built on the cowboy. Individuality, self-reliance, decency, and the desire to do the right thing. That tall, courageous, well-meaning hunk of man who was always there to take off his hat for ladies and save the good people from the bad people. You can't let the American cowboy just fall of the face of the earth."

Will stopped his speech and looked over at J.L. and the brunette, who were shooting pool again.

"J.L.," he said with a drunken slur, "don't you agree?"

"I agree," J.L. replied offhandedly. "It'll be a sad day for America when all the cowboys are gone."

He turned to the brunette.

"Eight ball, right corner," he said.

Lauren, Will, and the other cowboys watched him shoot. J.L. made a perfect cut in the designated pocket.

"You win again," she said, hanging up her cue stick.

"Where are you going?" J.L. asked.

"The powder room," she said. "Go ahead with your friends. I'll be back in a few."

"On your way back, get us a couple beers and we'll go sit outside again," he said, handing her some bills.

"Aye, aye, sir," she replied, saluting and taking the money.

J.L. hung up his cue and took a seat at the table with the Lazy B cowboys.

The table grew quiet.

"Where's my drink?" Will said. He looked over at the bartender. "Bring me another whiskey," he ordered, motioning to the bartender.

"Mr. Foreman!" Carlos pleaded. "You better take it easy. You been hitting that whiskey pretty hard."

"I know when I've had enough," Will said. With that, he got up from the table. "I'll be back," he said to the other cowboys. "Must relieve the stress on my urinary bladder."

He was unsteady as he turned and headed toward the restroom.

J.L. turned to Curly. "What are you going to do now?" he asked.

"Not sure," Curly said. "Me and Emily are going to get married and I don't know what I'll do then. I think I'll probably stay in the area. Emily's family is all here and she's not going to want to leave them." He took a swig of beer. "Whatever happens," Curly continued, "I'll survive. I'll eat and breathe fresh air and I'll have a good horse to ride somewhere."

J.L. nodded his approval. "What about you?" J.L. asked Carlos. "Where are you going from here?"

"Oh, Dios Mío," he said sadly, crossing himself. "God only knows. I can get a job cleaning tables at the El Torero over in White Fish. I can always go back to San Antonio and work with my brother in his auto body repair shop. I could go back and spend the rest of my days sanding down and painting cars."

"Good luck!" J.L. said, offering his hand.

"Thanks," Carlos said, grasping his hand tightly. "Good luck to you too."

J.L. looked over at Sonny. "What about you, Sonny?" J.L. asked.

Sonny looked downcast. He took a swig of beer and sat the bottle on the table. Then, his face screwed into an agonizing frown.

"All of my dreams are gone," he said sadly, trying to hold

back the tears. "All I ever wanted to do was ride the range, rope cattle, and be with other cowboys. I always wanted to be like J.L. and Curly and Will, and now I know it will never happen." Sonny stopped and then rested his head on his folded arms on the table and began sobbing uncontrollably.

"Come on, Sonny," J.L. said. "It's not that bad."

"Yes, it is," Sonny replied sadly. "Since I was six years old, the open range has been my life. I'm lost now. Oh God, I'm so lost right now." He put his head back down and continued to sob.

J.L. got up and put his hand on Sonny's shoulder. "I guess some of us were just born too late," he said consolingly. "It's a tragic thing. It really is. There's something out there for you; just wait and see."

"Thanks," Sonny said, wiping his tears on his shirtsleeve. "I hope so."

The table was quiet as the cowboys swigged their beer.

Curly turned to J.L. "What about you, J.L.?" he asked. "What are you going to do?"

"Not a hundred percent sure," J.L. replied. "I'm going to make a call to New York tomorrow and I'll see what happens."

"New York City?" Curly blurted out. "What's up there?"

Lauren appeared at the table with the beers and J.L. got up from the table and took one.

"I'll tell you later," he said. "I'm going outside with Lauren."

* * *

Moments later, J.L. and Lauren were seated again in the quietness of the evening on the back patio.

"You know, I really enjoy your company," she said, putting her hand on his knee. "I wanted you to come out here so we could talk in private."

J.L. could see she was very tipsy.

"Why don't you come spend some time with me tonight?" she continued, softly stroking the inside of his pants leg. "Back in my room, I've got two grams of top-shelf California snow."

J.L. laughed. "No, thanks," he said. "I don't mess with that stuff. I'll smoke a joint or drink a beer, but I'm afraid of that powder."

"J.L., what's wrong with you?" she asked pleadingly. "Look at this," she said, running her hands across her breasts and down to her thighs. "This is all woman."

"I'm flattered that you're so attracted to me," he said, "but...."

Seated across from him, she took his hands in hers and started rubbing them across her breasts.

"I need a man tonight," she said desperately. "To love me and hold me and bring out the woman in me."

"Whoa, whoa," he said quickly, pulling his hands away from hers and getting up from the table.

"What's wrong?" she asked, standing up to face him.

"I like you and I enjoy talking to you," he said, "but I don't go riding just any filly that comes into the pasture. At least, not 'til I get to know 'em."

She laughed. "You're old-fashioned," she said.

"Maybe I am," he replied, "but I'm not ready for all of that again. At least not yet."

"Are you still holding on to your dead wife?" she asked.

J.L. looked at her and said nothing. He was obviously annoyed that she would mention his dead wife in this context.

"J.L.!" he heard someone call.

He turned and saw Curly at the rear door.

"J.L.," Curly said, "Will is drunk as a skunk. We've got to get him back to the ranch."

"Be right in," J.L. replied.

Curly went back inside.

"Oh God! J.L.," she said, throwing her arms around his waist and hugging him tightly. "Please don't leave me with this terrible need tonight."

J.L. took her arms and unfolded them from around his waist.

"I'm sorry," he said. "I've got to go help Curly."

With that, he turned from her and went back inside the saloon.

***

Ten minutes later, J.L. and Curly, each with one of Will's arms around their necks, were physically carrying their dead-drunk foreman across the parking lot to J.L.'s truck. The brunette was in tandem, carrying a beer in one hand and Will's hat in the other.

Slowly but surely, J.L. and Curly lugged their foreman to the passenger side of J.L.'s pickup. J.L. opened the door and together they finally managed to get Will into the front seat. Curly got into the truck beside him and slammed the door.

"Here's his hat," the brunette said.

Curly took the hat and J.L. started around the truck to the driver's side. The brunette followed. As J.L. started to get in, she grabbed his arm.

"Yes?" J.L said, turning to face her.

"Why don't you like me?" she asked angrily. "I've got a lot of good things going for me."

"I've got to go," J.L. said, getting into the driver's side and slamming the door.

For a moment, she watched as J.L. started the engine. "You go to hell, cowboy!" she shouted in livid anger as the truck started to pull away. "You understand me? Go straight to hell!"

With that, she angrily threw the beer bottle at J.L.'s truck. It bounced off the rear fender as the vehicle pulled out of the parking lot.

***

The following morning, J.L. was waiting on the front porch of the bunkhouse when a Fedex truck pulled into the yard. The driver got out, handed a package to J.L., for which he signed, and the delivery truck pulled away.

J.L. opened the package.

Inside was a letter and two tickets. He read the letter:

To: Jerome Lafayette Crockett

32

C/O Lazy B Ranch
Lonesome Trail Road
Spokane, Washington 99212
Dear Mr. Crockett,

As per our oral agreement, you have been engaged by International Labor Services as a cattle maintenance employee at Rancho Palermo in Casa Grande, Argentina.

The first day of your employment, again as per our oral agreement, will be May 13, 2007, when you will report to Sr. Javier Gonzales, ranch foreman, to proceed with your duties.

Enclosed you will find two tickets for passage to said destination via La Senora, a vessel owned by South American Shipping Inc., based in Buenos Aires. Also enclosed you will find an itinerary and two tickets for you and your spouse on La Senora, a commercial vessel which will depart Miami, Florida, Pier 16 on May 8, 2007 at 12 noon. Please also find included two bus tickets via El Sol Autobus from Buenos Aires to Rancho Palermo. During said trip, all expenses will be paid by International Labor Services as per the agreement. Any further necessary expenses that might be incurred in completing said trip will be reimbursed by International Labor Services.

In the event Jerome Lafayette Crockett fails to report for duty on the agreed date, all stipulations of this contract will be null and void.

Upon receiving this package, please call toll-free at 1-800-783-0021 to confirm your reservation.

Sincerely,
International Labor Services,
322 East 56th Street
New York, N.Y. 10003

J.L. examined the tickets and smiled.

Looks like you're ready to go, he said to himself. *Put these tickets in a safe place and guard them with your life.* Suddenly, in his mind's eye, he saw himself walking up the gangplank of *La Senora* and waving good-bye to the people standing on the pier. He couldn't wait to get on the boat. It would be a new adventure in his life. He was ready. He needed a change.

Moments later, he was in the bunkhouse on the payphone.

"Operator, I want to make a call to New York..."

Exodus

Two days later, J.L.'s truck was parked in front of the ranch bunkhouse, loaded up for a trip. In the bed of the truck, an ice chest, a box of folded linens, and some tools had already been loaded. J.L. emerged from the front door with a suitcase in one hand and a small carrying bag in the other. Curly was behind him. At the truck, J.L. put the suitcase on the floorboard and the small bag in the front seat as Curly watched. Travel items securely stored, J.L. turned to Curly. "Check out my new nice chest," J.L. said, taking it out of the bed of the pickup and opening it for Curly. "Got it on sale for twelve bucks."

"It's a nice one," Curly said.

"There's something about new ice chests," he said, admiring the plastic box. "They turn me on."

Curly grinned.

J.L. reached in his pocket and pulled out a key. "Here's the key to the storage locker," J.L. said. "You and Emily make the most of all that stuff."

"We will," Curly said gratefully. "Thanks so much. I'll always remember you for helping us."

"I'm glad to help you," J.L. replied. "Remember, you got to have it empty before June first; that's when the lease expires. When I get to Argentina, I'll send you my address and I want you to send me some of those books. The primer on Freudian psychology, the poems of Gerard Manley Hopkins, the works of Aristotle and Plato—I'll send you a list."

"I'll take care of it," Curly replied. "You going to stop by St. Louis and visit Harold?"

"Yes," J.L. replied. "I'd love to see that crazy brother of

yours."

"Now don't forget that brother of mine has got some thieving ways," Curly said. "Don't trust him too far."

"Oh, I'm not worried about that," J.L. replied. "I've been too good a friend to him. He won't steal anything from me."

"I'm just telling you," Curly said.

They heard the door to the bunkhouse closing and turned to see Will walking down the bunkhouse steps toward them.

"What are you going to do now?" Will asked.

"I answered that ad in *American Cowboy*," J.L. replied. "I was just telling Curly about it."

"The one about going to Argentina?"

"Yep." J.L. nodded. "They overnighted me tickets, and I'm due to catch a ship out of Miami, Florida in nine days. It leaves at noon on April 23rd."

"Don't you think that's kind of a spur-of-the-moment decision?" Will asked.

J.L. looked at him.

"I'm a spur-of-the-moment kind of guy," he replied.

"In Argentina, they speak Spanish," Will said. "How are you going to communicate?"

"I'm going to learn," J.L. said. "I got tapes."

Will and Curly looked at him inquisitively.

"Hablo, hablas, habla, hablamos, habláis, hablan," J.L. replied.

Will and Curly looked at each other and laughed out loud.

"Well, good luck!" Will said, reaching in his pocket. He handed a small package to J.L., who looked at it curiously. "It's a credit card with $1,000 on it. Frank Jr. said he wanted to thank you for all your service. He says it was a going-away present."

"Tell him I said thanks," J.L. replied quietly.

"There's a password to use it," Will said. "The password is the last four numbers of your social security number."

"I'll remember that," J.L. said.

J.L. turned to Curly. They looked at each other for a long wistful moment. "I guess this is goodbye, old friend," J.L.

said.

"Yeah, I guess so," Curly said. They shook hands.

"I'll write you when I get to Argentina."

Curly nodded his approval. "Tell Harold I said hello."

"I will," J.L. said. He turned to Will.

"It's been eight years," Will said wistfully. "It's been a good eight years."

"Yes, it has," J.L. said sadly. "Thanks so much for making it so great for me."

They shook hands and hugged one another.

"Goodbye!" Will said.

"So long," J.L. said sadly and started for his truck.

J.L. took about six steps toward the truck and Will called his name.

"You know you'll be the last cowboy on this earth," Will said. "After computers and Easy-Herd and satellites have put all the other cowboys out of work, you'll still be riding the range somewhere."

"I hope so," J.L. replied. "It's all I ever loved."

He looked at his old friends one more time as he opened the door and got into the pickup. "I'll miss you guys," he said sadly. "You'll hear from me once I get settled in Argentina."

Will and Curly waved a final goodbye and watched as J.L. started the engine. Moments later, the truck headed down the ranch driveway for the last time and then turned on the main highway.

***

Two miles outside of town, J.L. maneuvered the pickup off the main highway and up the hill past the church to the cemetery he and Curly had visited earlier in the week. Near the top of the hill, the pickup stopped under the shade of several aspens. As before, he got out and walked to his wife's grave. For a moment, he stared at the headstone. Then, he took off his hat and bowed his head sadly. After another moment of silence, he raised his head and looked across the cemetery.

"I'm leaving," he said finally, his voice breaking. "I'm leaving Washington State and the Lazy B and Curly and Rebel and Will and—you."

He broke down in heart-wrenching sobs.

"And I'm leaving all of this," he said almost in anger, motioning to the mountains and the trees and the sky.

"All the things we had, I'm leaving behind," he said. "There is no way I can take it with me."

He stopped for a moment and then he started pacing back and forth in front of the grave.

"The old grandfather clock that belonged to your mother, I gave it to the Salvation Army. And the shamrock medallion that you won at the State Fair in Salt Lake, I gave to your friend Martha Hancock. Remember her? She's the woman that made all of the boysenberry jelly for us.

"All the rest of our stuff—the old oak table and chairs and the bed and the chest of drawers we bought from the Woodalls—I gave to Curly. He's about to get married and he and his new wife will need it. I'm going down to Miami, Florida to get on a boat and see where it takes me. They say it's going to Argentina to a cattle ranch. We'll see. As usual, I don't know where my life is going," he said with a muffled laugh. "Of course, you've always known that. Remember when we threw everything in my pickup in Durango and left Colorado to come to Washington State?" he said with a muffled laugh. "I didn't even tell the foreman I was leaving. Remember that? We didn't know where we were going then. I guess some things never change.

"In my heart, I know I'll never be back this way again. I just wanted to say goodbye."

He stopped again.

"It's time for me to start over," he said. "I'm sure you understand. You understood me better than anybody else on this earth. That's why I'll always love you."

He stopped and drew a deep breath. He drew his shirtsleeve across his face to wipe away the tears and looked at the gravestone one last time. Then, he quickly turned from the grave, replaced his black hat, and headed briskly to the pickup without looking back.

As the truck's engine roared to life, J.L. Crockett had the look of a man who was determined to start a new life. In a cloud of dust, the old pickup rumbled back down the hillside and turned back on the highway. It was one hour to Interstate 90 East.

DeWayne

Following I-90 east from Spokane Valley, J.L. cruised into Idaho and soon started the tortuous climb through the Bitterroot Mountains, winding up and down and all around through the narrow mountain passes. Near the top of the range, he crossed into Montana. Then, he made the slow, winding descent back down the east side of the Bitterroots to the sprawling open plains of southern Montana. Over the next few hours, he passed through a succession of nondescript Montana towns. As his pickup cruised eastward, he gazed out at the open plains on either side of the truck and tried to imagine what it looked like when these lands were populated with native Indians and their cooking fires, drying skins, teepees, and ponies. This was the land of the Crow, the Northern Cheyenne, the Arapaho, and the Lakota Sioux.

On his map, he had marked the places he wanted to stop and visit on his way to Miami. He planned his first stop to be at Hardin, Montana, a small town east of Billings where he would get a motel for the night. According to plan, he would get up early the next day and do the tour of Little Big Horn at Crow Agency. He had read extensively about Custer's Last Stand, but he wanted to see the actual battleground for himself and gain a better understanding of exactly what had happened between Yellow Hair and Crazy Horse.

Inside the truck, he tried to entertain himself. He chewed gum, listened to the Spanish tapes, and played a medley of Slim Whitman's old Western songs. There was "Ghosts Riders in the Sky," "Tumbling Tumbleweeds," "Sweet Maria," and "On the Sunny Side of the Rockies." He knew it was going to be a long trip; he had to make it as enjoyable as possible.

As planned, he arrived in Hardin by nightfall and got a small motel room just outside of town. He had a hamburger and fries and gassed up his truck for the following morning. Back at the hotel, he watched TV for a while and then showered and was in bed by 8:30.

Promptly at 9:00 the next morning, J.L.'s pickup pulled into the parking lot at the Little Big Horn monument in Crow Agency and took a parking spot beside a tourist bus. As he walked to the entrance, he could see a shuttered museum and tour guides inside a closed area, getting ready to start their day. Along the sidewalk leading to the ticket office, there were several street entertainers present to occupy visitors while they waited for the museum and ticket office to open. There was already a long line of tourists to buy tickets. J.L. took a place at the end of the line and glanced over at the entertainers.

Among the entertainers were a contortionist, a juggler, a man playing a guitar, and a sidewalk preacher. Beside the sidewalk preacher, there was an old Indian man sitting on a portable tree stump with a sign tacked to it. The old Indian, dressed in native garb with a headband, some feathers, and his gray hair done in long pigtails, was sitting perfectly still on the tree stump, staring stoically straight ahead. J.L. looked at the sign. *I am Chief Lone Wolf, the last surviving great-grandson of the great Apache Chief Geronimo. I have been driven from the lands of my people and left to seek refuge in the modern world of the white eyes. Your donations are appreciated.*

Surrounding the sign, there were photos of a young Indian boy beside an older Indian man with two ponies and a teepee in the background. In his hand, the old Indian held an aging black felt hat that served as a donation receptacle.

"Young fellow, do you know the love of Jesus Christ?" the street preacher called to one of the tourists. The preacher, waving a Bible in his right hand, was a baby-faced fat man in his late thirties in an ill-fitting shirt and with a strong southern accent.

"It is a love that can save your soul from the bottomless pits of perdition. It is a love that transports you beyond this world of sin and suffering and presents to you the eternal glory of ever-lasting life. This great book that I hold in my hand is the key to knowing your Lord and Savior Jesus Christ."

The tourist who was being addressed looked away disinterestedly.

J.L. glanced over at the street preacher.

"Tell me, my brother," the fat preacher said, turning to J.L. "Do you know the great love of Jesus Christ?"

J.L., noticing that the museum was now opening and the crowd was starting to move, smiled politely at the street preacher and then turned to move with the ticket line.

***

Twenty minutes later, J.L. and an assortment of tourists, some thirty to forty strong, were strolling along the grassy knoll beyond the museum and listening to their tour guide.

"Now here is where Custer and his men made their final stand," the guide, a youngish, plain-looking woman in glasses with a bookish look, explained. "Twenty-five-thousand savage Indians—Sioux, Cheyenne, Arapaho, and Crow—charged down upon them from the hills over there," she said, pointing to the northwest. "Although Custer and his cavalrymen were outnumbered ten to one, they fought bravely. They shot their horses and used them for breastworks. After they ran out of ammunition, they resorted to knives and the butts of their rifles to repel the savage Indians. Bloody but unbowed, they fought courageously to the very last man. These were the brave men of the seventh cavalry," she said in conclusion. "They all died heroic deaths."

She paused and then asked, "Any questions?"

"Why did the Indians want to kill Custer and his men?" asked a young white woman in a chartreuse top and paisley slacks.

"Because they were savage Indians," the guide said self-righteously. "They had never known civilized society. They were like animals. They didn't understand the rule of law and order. They were vermin with no real emotions."

She stopped.

"Bull! That's not the reason," J.L. blurted out. "It was payback time."

Everyone in the crowd turned to face J.L.

"The Indians wiped them out because Custer and his men had slaughtered innocent Indian women and children in raids all across the west. These people had a way of life here. They weren't savage, lawless animals. They had a code of ethics and a crude legal system. They wanted to live in peace and prosper and raise their children just like the white man. They had lived on these lands for thousands of years. Custer was the savage. He was the blood-thirsty one that took no prisoners and, when he and his men were killed here, they got what was coming to them."

The stunned tour guide didn't reply at first. Then, she screwed up her face and glared angrily at J.L.

"You don't know your history, mister," she shot back. "I've read thirteen books on the history of Custer's campaign in the West, and I can tell you that he and his men didn't deserve to be slaughtered."

"I've read several books on Custer," J.L. said. "But I've tried to derive some truth from my reading. All you've learned is to follow the party line of the white man."

The woman glared again at J.L., then she composed herself and turned to the other visitors. "Are there any more questions?" she asked politely.

There was total silence.

"Okay, that's the end of the tour," the guide said sweetly. "I hoped you enjoyed it. Please follow the trail back down to the museum."

With that, the crowd dispersed and started walking back down the hill.

The tour guide made a beeline for J.L.

"Look, mister," she said angrily. "We don't like troublemakers. We run a clean operation here for the tour-going public."

"You could tell the truth," J.L. said.

The tour guide turned huffily from J.L and briskly walked

away.

As the crowd followed the winding trail across the grassy knoll back to the museum, J.L. took a short cut and hurried back to the museum. He wanted to get back on the road.

***

Ten minutes later, he was back at the museum and several minutes ahead of the other tourists. At the entrance, all of the street entertainers were gone except for the fat street preacher and the old Indian.

As J.L. approached, the preacher called to him.

"Is the tour over?" he asked.

J.L. nodded.

"Can you help me with him?" the preacher asked, indicating the old Indian man, who was resting on a folding recliner.

"Sure," J.L. said and walked over.

"Let's get him back on the stump," the preacher ordered.

The preacher raised the old Indian up to a sitting position on the recliner. With the preacher on one side and J.L. on the other, they helped him to his feet and slowly walked him over to the stump where the marquee was located. Slowly and carefully, they lowered him into a seated position on the stump.

"Thanks, cowboy," the preacher said.

"No problem," J.L. said.

By now, the tourists had arrived back at the entrance and were milling around, waiting for the tour bus to come pick them up. J.L. watched as several tourists stopped and peered curiously at the old Indian man, their interest in him apparently whetted by the tour.

The old Indian slowly raised his hand in a prophetic gesture.

"Since many, many moons, my people lived peacefully on these lands and raised their families by killing the buffalo. Then, the white eyes came and buffalo all gone. Slowly but surely, the white man killed away the great buffalo that had fed and clothed my people for many, many moons. After

44

buffalo gone, we have no food during cold winter and we must eat rat."

He stopped.

"Oh no!" a middle-aged, overweight woman with lots of jewelry, a designer handbag, and expensive sunglasses said sympathetically. "You had to eat rats?"

The old Indian nodded sadly.

"You ever eat rat?" he asked, looking directly into the woman's eyes.

"Oh no!" she said, withdrawing in horror. "I've never eaten rat."

Almost twenty tourists were now listening intently to the old Indian.

"During cold winters, the old people and babies starve. Mothers cry loudly when they bury their little ones in cold ground to send them to Happy Hunting Ground. Indians very sad. Indians feel Great Spirit has gone away—" Suddenly, the old Indian stopped.

As the tourists watched, his hand fell to his side. He started gasping for breath. Then, he grimaced in pain, clutched his chest, and fell off the stump to the ground. The hat with the donations fell to the ground with the old Indian.

The tourists withdrew in horror.

The street preacher rushed over and picked up the hat.

"Stand back! Stand back!" the fat preacher ordered, fanning the prostrate Indian with a bible and holding the hat in the other. "He is old and frail. Give him some air! Give him some air!"

"Oh, poor thing!" one woman said, dropping a twenty-dollar bill in the hat.

"Oh, I hope he'll be okay," another woman said, dropping several bills into the hat.

"Me too!" said a tall, middle-aged man in a planter's hat, peeling off several bills from a fat wad and dropping them into the hat. "It's a shame the way we've treated these poor people."

"That poor Indian!" said another tourist, placing more

money in the hat. "I've got to do something."

By now, all the tourists were standing in line with donation money in hand.

"God bless y'all! God bless y'all," the fat preacher said to the chorus of donors dropping bills into the hat. "Chief Lone Wolf appreciates your generosity."

By now, the hat was full of bills.

Moments later, as J.L. watched, the tour bus arrived and all of the tourists scrambled to get onboard. Then, in a cloud of thick diesel smoke, the tourist bus pulled away and left J.L., the fat preacher, and the old Indian to themselves.

"Hey, cowboy," the preacher said. "Can you help me get him to the van?"

J.L. bent down over the old Indian and pulled his left arm around his neck and the preacher did the same with the other arm.

Together, each struggling to support the old Indian, they started walking him toward an old blue van parked nearby.

When they arrived, the preacher opened the passenger side door and J.L. tried to hold him up. Suddenly, the old Indian became alive. He saw J.L.

"Turn loose of me, you sonuvabitch," the old Indian said angrily, jerking his arm out of J.L.'s grasp.

"Chief! Chief!" the preacher admonished. "Calm down! This man is trying to help you."

"Where's the money?" he demanded. "Where's the God-damn money?"

"It's inside the van in the hat," the preacher replied.

The old Indian looked inside the van, saw the hat filled with bills, and took it in his hand.

"Someday, I open casino in Cabazon," he said, feeling the money between his fingers. "I be rich redskin then."

He looked back at J.L.

"Stay away from me, you sonuvabitch," he said angrily.

J.L. backed away.

"Come on, fat-ass," the old Indian said, clutching the money-filled hat to his bosom. "Let's get out of here."

The preacher looked apologetically at J.L. and then turned back to the Indian.

"Can you wait right here while I get the props?" the preacher asked.

"Hurry up!" the old Indian shouted. "I ain't got all day."

Inside the van, J.L. noticed stacks upon stacks of Bibles. There were also several Indian costumes, blankets, and a fake buffalo head.

Moments later, the fat street preacher reappeared. In one hand, he had the fake tree stump and, in the other, the marquee with the photos and the text.

"Hey, cowboy," the preacher said, hastily throwing the sign and the fake tree stump into the back of the van. "I appreciate your help."

"I hope he'll be okay," J.L. said.

"He'll be all right," the preacher said. "What's your name?"

"J.L.," he replied. "What's yours?"

"DeWayne," the preacher said. "DeWayne Carter. Maybe I'll see you again."

With that, the fat preacher got into the blue van with the Bibles and the old Indian and slammed the door. He waved goodbye and the old van pulled out of the gravel parking lot in a cloud of dust and sped off onto the highway.

The Meeting

As planned, J.L. left Crow Agency promptly at 10:30 a.m. Back on Interstate 90 and cruising east again, he was still trying to entertain himself. His new ice chest was in the passenger seat beside him. Inside, there were bottled waters and sandwiches. Also in the seat were nine packages of Fancy Fruit chewing gum, a bag of potato chips, his maps, and a hard-back copy of *The Wonders of Argentina*. As he cruised through the rolling open plains of southeastern Montana, he sipped bottled water. His next stop was Rapid City, South Dakota, where he planned to stop at Mount Rushmore. He figured about two hundred miles to Rapid City and, if all went well, he would arrive there around 1:30 that afternoon.

An hour later, he crossed the Montana state line and entered South Dakota. For the first time, he saw the Black Hills; so named because the trees are so green they appear black. After he was about thirty miles into South Dakota, he heard the sudden squeal of a police siren behind him and pulled over to the side of the highway. It was the South Dakota Highway Patrol. *Just what I need*, he thought as he watched the officer approach in his rear view mirror. *A speeding ticket.*

"License and registration, please," the policeman said.

J.L. retrieved the documents and handed them to the policeman.

"Be right back," the officer said, returning to the patrol car.

As J.L. watched in his rear view mirror, he could see the officer running his information. Finally, the officer returned.

"You know you were doing seventy-four in a seventy-mile-an-hour zone," he said.

"Yes, sir," J.L. replied. "I wasn't watching my speedometer very closely."

"I'm going to give you a warning," the officer said. "In the future, watch your speed."

"I will," J.L. promised.

Ten minutes later, the officer appeared again and handed J.L. the warning ticket.

"Thanks for the consideration," J.L. said, taking the ticket.

"You know the state of Illinois has a fugitive warrant out for a Jerome L. Crockett."

"Really?" J.L. said.

"The guy the warrant is out for is a Jerome Lafollette Crockett. Your birthday and his are slightly different, but the names are very similar," the officer said.

"What's he wanted for?" J.L. asked.

"Murder and armed robbery."

"That's a serious charge."

"You betcha," the officer said.

"Okay. Thanks for the info," J.L. said.

"Have a good day," the officer said.

J.L. watched as the officer returned to the patrol car and then sped off down the highway.

Moments later, J.L. was cruising down I-90 again. Inside the truck, he finished another bottle of water and absently tossed the plastic bottle into the passenger side floorboard. There were already several empty plastic bottles in the passenger floorboard. He reached into the ice chest and pulled out a fresh water and started sipping.

As he drove, he wondered how gauchos threw the bolas to bring down a steer or calf. There had to be a special skill to that, he thought, like an American cowboy learning to tie and throw a lariat. He wondered if there were any differences between the way horses were saddled in Argentina. Did they use a cinch and a bellyband? He was anxious to get started on his new adventure.

For several minutes, he rode quietly. Finally, bored, he put the Spanish tape into the player.

"Estar is the Spanish verb that denotes state of being," the narrator said. "The six words in the declension are estoy, estás, está, estamos, estáis, están."

"Estoy, estás, está, estamos, estáis, están," J.L. repeated over and over to himself trying to capture the exact pronunciation of the words. "Estoy, estás, está, estamos...."

***

At 1:11 p.m., J.L. arrived in Rapid City. As he rounded the curve on Interstate 90 and looked up to see the faces on Mount Rushmore, all he saw were giant sheets of material covering the faces of Washington and Jefferson. For a moment, he couldn't believe his eyes. The faces of Teddy Roosevelt and Lincoln were evident, but what appeared to be giant sheets of gray canvas obscured the faces of Washington and Jefferson. *What the hell is that all about?* he wondered. *They must be doing maintenance or something.*

As he neared the commercial district of Rapid City, he stopped to gas up. As he pulled in, he noticed the sign over the station was swinging back and forth in the strong winds for which the area was famous. Once he stopped in front of a gas pump, he could see the winds blowing trash and pieces of paper across the concrete apron of the station. In the bay in front of his truck, a smallish, dark-haired woman had the gas on automatic pumping and was cleaning the windshield of an old sedan with an Oregon plate. As she reached back to replace the wiper in the bucket, the high winds sent the bucket tumbling end-over-end across the pumping area.

Instinctively, J.L. opened the door and jumped out to help. Holding his hat against the wind, he gave chase after the errant bucket. Finally, the wind blew the bucket against a fence and it stopped. J.L. grabbed it and started walking back to the pumps. He handed it to the woman and she replaced it on the pier.

"Thank you!" she said gratefully. "This wind is a lot faster than I am."

"You're welcome," he said, turning to go inside the station

office.

Inside, he asked the clerk, a middle-aged, balding man with a mustache, why the faces on Mount Rushmore were covered.

"The National Association of Black People is holding a convention here this week. They got a court order to have the faces of Washington and Jefferson covered. They said they were offensive."

"Offensive?" J.L. asked, gathering food items from the station's cooler.

"They said Washington and Jefferson were slave holders and they were offended by their presence," the clerk replied. "They did it. The faces will be covered for another week."

J.L. shook his head in sheer disgust. If he couldn't see all of the faces as anticipated, he wouldn't see any of them. *So much for Mount Rushmore*, he thought. He placed several food items on the counter.

"I want to pay for these and get forty-five dollars on number seven," J.L. said, handing the clerk some bills.

"You got it," the clerk said, punching some keys on the register.

Fifteen minutes later, J.L. was back in the truck heading east on I-90. His gas tank was filled to the brim. He was armed with two fried chicken sandwiches, a six-pack of soft drinks, two jumbo bags of potato chips, and eight packs of Fancy Fruit chewing gum. He was armed for the onslaught.

About fifteen miles outside of Rapid City, there was a sudden change of scenery. From the lush green for which the Black Hills were famous, the landscape became a passing portrait of naked, multi-hued earthen structures made up of endlessly eroded buttes, pinnacles, and spires blended with mixed-grass prairie. These were the Badlands of South Dakota.

Inside the truck, J.L. was still trying to entertain himself. For several minutes, he listened to the Spanish tapes and then he turned on the radio. Bored with the local news, he changed the station and then slowed when he saw what appeared to be a stalled car on the side of the road ahead of him. As he approached, he noticed it was the same old sedan with an Oregon plate he had seen the dark-haired woman driving at the service station. He pulled off the highway and got out of the truck.

The moment he got out of the truck, he grabbed his black hat so the high winds that were whipping about would not blow it off his head. He could see that the woman was out of her car and standing in front of it with the hood open.

"Oh, thank you, thank you!" she said gratefully, turning to greet him. "Please help me! I don't know anything about cars."

"Let me have a look," J.L. said.

J.L. stuck his head under the hood. He took the breather off and flipped the carburetor's butterfly a couple times.

"It's not getting gas," he said expertly. "I think it's the fuel pump. Let me run a little test. I always carry an extra gallon of gas."

"Are you sure you know what you're doing?" she asked.

"Of course," he replied. "I used to be a mechanic."

"Thank goodness," she said.

Still holding his black hat against the high winds, J.L. walked to his truck and, moments later, returned with a small gas can.

"I'm going to prime the carburetor," he said. "Get inside and try to start it when I tell you."

Obediently, the woman got inside the car.

J.L. poured a small amount of gas into the throat of the carburetor.

"Okay, hit it," he ordered.

She turned the ignition. The car's engine ground over and over again without starting.

He stuck his head under the hood again and poured more gas into the carburetor.

"Okay, try it again!" he instructed.

She turned the ignition again and the car's engine area exploded in flames.

"Oh my God! Oh my God!" she said, opening up the car door and jumping out.

For a moment, J.L. was speechless as he looked at the burning car.

"Look what you did to my car!" she screamed at him angrily. "Oh God!" she screamed in horror. "I've got to get my purse and my suitcase."

She rushed toward the burning car. J.L. rushed forward and grabbed her arm. "Stay here!" he ordered. "I'll get it!"

In a flash, he rushed to the car, opened the door, and retrieved a woman's purse from the front seat. The flames and smoke were growing heavier.

"Where's the suitcase?" he called to her, waving his hand to ward off the smoke and flames.

"In the back seat!" she screamed.

Quickly, he opened the back door of the vehicle, grabbed a single suitcase, and fled the burning vehicle. When J.L. was no more than fifteen feet away with the purse and suitcase in hand, the car exploded in a giant ball of flames.

For several moments, J.L. and the woman stood dumbfounded, watching the flames, fed by the whipping high winds, consume the automobile. Finally, they looked at one another.

"You crazy cowboy!" she screamed at him in horrified anger. "I don't have a car! Five minutes ago, I had a car. Now I don't have a car. You crazy cowboy, you crazy, crazy cowboy," she shouted.

She rushed at him with girlish fists and started pounding his chest.

"Whoa, whoa! Hang on now!" he said, grabbing her hands and holding them defensively. "I was just trying to help."

"Oh yeah," she said sarcastically. "You helped, all right. You destroyed my car. Look at that!" she shouted, pointing to the smoking, still-ablaze hull of the old sedan. "Now what am I going to do?

"I'm not sure," J.L. said. "Let's see if we can figure this thing out."

"You destroyed my car and you're not sure," she shouted in livid anger. "You better come up with something and it'd better be quick. I have no transportation. How am I ever going to get to my aunt's house with no car? Tell me that, cowboy! What do I do now?"

J.L. didn't know what to say.

"Look, I'm sorry. I was only trying to help," he said apologetically. "Let's figure this thing out."

"Figure it out? You lunatic! Look at that!" she shouted, pointing again to the burned-out shell that was once her car. "What is there to figure out?"

"You've got to stay calm," he said. "We'll never figure it out if you don't stay calm."

She stared first at the burning car, then at J.L. Suddenly, in pure outrage, she slammed the suitcase to the ground. It popped open and women's clothing started flying about in the whipping winds. Two dresses, a pair of jeans, several undergarments, and a jacket blew out of the suitcase.

"Oh my God! Oh my God!" she screamed, realizing what she had done. She hastily started trying to gather up the garments.

A white brassiere blew into J.L.'s face and the straps wrapped around his neck. Delicately, he removed it.

"Give me that!!" she shouted angrily. She snatched the brassiere out of his hand.

Finally, after several minutes, she gathered up all of the garments and returned them to her suitcase. Then, suitcase in hand, she started walking down the highway away from J.L. Finally, about fifty yards away, she took a seat on the suitcase, put her face in her hands, and started crying.

J.L. walked to her. She looked up from her crying, saw him, and screamed, "Get away from me! Get as far away from me as you can. You've caused enough trouble today!"

For a moment, J.L. said nothing. "Look!" he said finally. "Please let me help you! I'm terribly sorry about what happened. I can take you back to Rapid City to make a phone call or do whatever you need to do....Do you have insurance?"

"No," she said. "It expired two weeks ago. I've been trying to save my money."

Now she had had enough. She stood up. With her suitcase in one hand and holding out the thumb of her other hand to passing cars, she started walking down the highway away from J.L. Several cars zoomed by.

"Why won't you let me help you?" he said. "I know I'm responsible for your car, but I'll be glad to help any way I can...."

She looked away.

"Can we please talk?" he asked.

She opened her purse, took out a handkerchief, and started wiping her eyes.

"Can we talk?" J.L. asked again.

She smiled faintly. She could see he wasn't going away.

"One thing I'll say for you, cowboy," she said. "You don't give up."

"Look," he said. "Let me help you. Where are you going?"

"I'm going to St. Louis," she said.

"That's right on my route," he said. "I'll be happy take you to St. Louis. Once we're there, I take you directly to the place you want to go. No strings attached. You can call for help or call friends or relatives or do whatever you need to do. I feel terrible about all of this."

She looked at him and then she looked away thoughtfully. Finally, she turned back to him.

"Okay," she said finally. "I really don't have much choice."

She gave a resigned sigh, got up, and took her suitcase.

"Thank you," J.L. said. "Now you're making some sense."

"I'm just going with you to St. Louis," she warned. "That's it, so don't be getting any ideas about me, okay?"

"I'm not getting any ideas," J.L. said innocently.

Together, they walked back to J.L.'s truck. J.L. stopped.

"Are we going to just leave the car on the side of the road like this?"

"What else can we do?" she said. "It's no good to anybody now."

J.L. shrugged.

"Okay," he said. "I guess the state will haul it away. Come on; let's go."

Once they reached the truck, J.L. started to open the door.

"I can get my own door," she said sharply.

"Suit yourself," he said.

She opened the door and several empty plastic water bottles fell out on the ground. Instantly, the wind scattered them along the roadside. J.L. rushed to gather them up. Moments later, he stuffed them inside a plastic shopping bag and placed the bag inside the truck.

"Sorry," he said.

She got into the truck and slammed the door.

J.L. walked around the truck and got into the driver's seat.

"Is everything okay now?" he asked.

"Oh, everything is just hunky-dory," she said sarcastically. "I've never been so happy in my entire life."

Karina

Ten minutes later, J.L. and his passenger were cruising eastward on I-90. Inside the truck, they were separated in the front seat by the ice chest. She was uncomfortably cramped between the ice chest to her left and her suitcase in her lap. As they rode, she stared stoically straight ahead at the highway. Now that she was in the truck, he looked over at her, examining her closely for the first time. She was short, maybe five-foot-four, in her late twenties, with flowing black hair, a thin face, narrow nose, and full lips. She appeared Spanish or Latin of some description, he thought, probably Italian, although there was no trace of an accent in her voice. *Not bad looking either,* he thought.

She sensed that he was staring at her. She turned and glared angrily out of her large, brown eyes. "What are you looking at?" she snapped. "Haven't you ever seen a woman before?"

"Why are you sulled up like a mad heifer?" he shot back. "Neither one of us can change what happened back there."

"What did you call me?" she asked. "A heffer? What's a heffer?"

"A heifer," he replied, "is a young cow that has never been bred."

"So I'm a cow?" she replied angrily.

"I didn't say you were a cow," he replied apologetically. "I was speaking metaphorically."

"That's what it sounded like," she replied angrily.

"Forget it!" he said. "I didn't mean any harm."

"Just get this cow to St. Louis," she said angrily. "That's all l want from you. Do that and you'll never see me again."

She turned from him, suitcase still in her lap, and stared straight ahead at the highway.

They rode quietly for some fifteen minutes.

"Can I at least ask your name?" he asked finally.

"No!" she snapped back.

J.L. shook his head resignedly.

"I've heard about Italian spitfires, but you take the cake."

"What makes you think I'm Italian?" she shot back.

"What nationality are you?"

"None of your business!"

J.L. inhaled resignedly again and remained silent.

On the truck's CD player, Slim Whitman sang, "I Remember You!" in his time-honored melodic yodel.

"Look," he said calmly. "I'll be happy to take you to wherever you're going in St Louis. But it will be tomorrow night before we get there. Meanwhile, why can't we show one another all due honor and respect?"

"What are you trying to say?"

"We can at least be civil with one another."

"I don't want to be civil with you," she snapped. "You destroyed my car. Just get me to St. Louis!"

J.L. turned his attention back to driving.

"There are soft drinks and sandwiches in the cooler if you want any," he said.

"I'm not hungry," she said coldly.

"I was just trying to show some consideration."

"Don't worry about considering me," she said. "Just get me to St. Louis."

They rode silently.

"Do you mind if I play my Spanish tapes?"

"It's your truck," she said.

J.L. started the Spanish tapes.

"Cómo está?" the narrator said. "How are you?"

"Cómo está?" J.L. repeated in his southern Texas drawl.

"Quieres ir conmigo?" the narrator said. "Do you want to go with me?"

"Quieres ir conmigo," J.L. repeated. "Quieres ir conmigo.

Quieres ir conmigo," he repeated over and over.

For almost an hour, they rode silently; the only sounds were J.L. repeating Spanish phrases and the constant quiet roar of the truck's engine as it cruised eastward on Interstate 90.

"Sioux Falls is just ahead," J.L. said finally. "I'm going to stop and use the restroom."

"I need a charger for my cell phone," she said.

"What happened to the old one?"

"Well, you see," she said sarcastically, "this crazy cowboy stopped to help me with my car. Not only did the car burn up, but the charger burned up with it."

J.L. sighed. "I'm sorry," he said.

"Would you be kind enough to let me use the cigarette lighter in your truck to charge my cell phone?"

"No problem," J.L. said.

"Thank you," she said coldly.

***

Twenty minutes later, J.L.'s truck pulled out of a service station on the outskirts of Sioux Falls. J.L. had used the restroom, she bought a phone charger, and they were on the road again. Some six miles east, J.L. left Interstate 90 and turned southeast on Interstate 29, straddling the state line between Iowa and Nebraska. Inside, J.L.'s passenger was still scrunched up next to the ice chest with her suitcase in her lap and her cell phone charging in the truck's ignition. J.L. changed the tape in the truck's cassette player. Some ten minutes later, she glanced down at the charger.

"Thank God!" she said, looking down at the charger and seeing that the phone was charged. "I can get connected to the outside world again."

With that, she disconnected the charger, dialed a number, and waited for the answer.

"Bueno," she said. "Puedo hablar con la señora Marta Escobedo?"

There was a pause.

"Hola, Mamacita," she said.

Then she looked at J.L.

"Cowboy," she said, "can you stop the truck so I can talk to my mother?"

"Why do I need to stop the truck?"

"Because I want my privacy," she said.

"You're speaking Spanish," he said. "I don't know what you are saying anyway."

"I'm not taking any chances," she said.

J.L. sighed and pulled the truck off to the side of the interstate and stopped.

"Thank you," she said coldly and then got out of the truck and continued her conversation.

For some ten minutes, J.L. sat quietly in the truck, listening to the Spanish tapes and watching other vehicles whiz past on the interstate. Finally, her conversation finished, she returned to the truck.

"Okay," she announced. "We can go now."

J.L. looked at her with a peeved expression, said nothing, and pulled back out on the highway.

They rode silently for several minutes; the only sound was the roar of the truck's engine and the droning of the Spanish tape.

Her cell phone rang again.

"Bueno!" she said.

For an instant, she turned from the cell phone and looked at J.L.

"Okay, okay," he said. "I'll stop again."

Again, he pulled the truck to the side of the highway and stopped. Again, she got out to talk and J.L. sat silently in the truck, listening to the droning Spanish tape and the passing vehicles.

Finally, she returned to the truck.

"That's the last time I'm stopping," he said. "Let me get you to St. Louis and you can talk on your phone and have all the privacy you want. Okay?"

She looked at him defensively.

"Is the cowboy putting his foot down?"

"Yes." J.L. replied firmly. "The cowboy is putting his foot

down. The cowboy has got to get on down the road."

They rode silently.

Finally, she looked over at him.

"I'm sorry, cowboy," she said calmly. "When everything is considered, you've been very good."

He looked over at her. "I'll have you in St. Louis tomorrow afternoon and you can go your own way, okay?"

She didn't reply.

Now J.L.'s truck was cruising through the open plains of central Kansas. On either side of the highway, he could see the fallow wheat fields stretching to the horizon, waiting to be planted for the new season.

"I've still got an extra chicken sandwich if you'd like one," he said.

She looked at him.

"What's on it?"

"Mayonnaise, lettuce, tomatoes, and chicken."

"Is it warm?"

"No, it's cold," he said. "I bought it this morning."

She looked at him.

"I think I'll have it," she said.

With his free hand, he opened the door to the ice chest between them and handed her the sandwich.

"Want a soft drink?"

"Yes, please."

He handed her a soft drink.

"There are some chips," he said, indicating a giant bag with the top rolled up in the seat between them.

She unwrapped the sandwich and started eating. After two bites, she reached for the potato chips.

For some fifteen minutes, they cruised down Interstate 29 while she ate and Slim Whitman wailed away on his classic tune, "On the Sunny Side of the Rockies."

"Okay, cowboy," she said finally, "Maybe you're right. We should be nice to one another. Let's call a truce."

"Thanks!" he replied.

"But don't be getting any ideas about me," she snapped

back. "I'm small, but I'm tough."

"Okay, okay," he conceded. "I'm not getting any ideas. I wouldn't dare get any ideas," he added sarcastically.

"My name is Karina," she said. "Karina Escobedo Leyva Gonzales Cruz.

J.L. grimaced.

"What?"

"Karina Escobedo Leyva Gonzales Cruz," she said again.

"Why do you have so many names?" he asked.

"That's a long story," she said. "What's your name?"

"I'm J.L. Crockett," he replied. "Pleased to meet you."

"Thank you!" she said. "Pleased to meet you."

She was much calmer now.

"I'm sorry about what happened back there," he said.

"It's okay," she said. "The mechanic in Portland said the fuel pump he installed was a used one. I know you were trying to be helpful."

"You lived in Portland?"

"There you go, asking questions again."

"I'm just trying to make conversation."

She sighed and then turned back to him.

"I lived outside Portland in a little town called Lake Oswego."

"I've heard of the town," he said. "What kind of work did you do?"

"I was a hairdresser."

"You worked in a beauty shop?"

"Yes," she said, "Can we change the subject?"

He knew that was the signal that he was asking too many questions

They rode quietly.

Outside, darkness had fallen across the Kansas countryside.

"We'll be in Kansas City in about two hours," he said. "What about the sleeping arrangements?"

"Sleeping arrangements?"

"You do plan on sleeping tonight. Right?"

"I hadn't thought about it," she said. "So what can you offer? Remember, you promised to get me to St. Louis safe and sound."

"I know and I'll live up to my promise," he said. "I can't afford two rooms."

She looked at him, saying nothing.

"I'll get a room for you and I'll sleep in the truck," he suggested.

She continued to study him and didn't reply.

"You really do want to do the right thing, don't you?" she said finally.

"I like to think of myself as a fair person."

"Okay," she said. "We can get a room together, but I want my privacy. Get a room with two beds and we'll hang a sheet between the beds so we can each have our privacy."

"We can do that," he said. "Please rest assured that I'll respect your privacy."

She didn't answer.

***

An hour later, J.L.'s truck pulled into a small motel on the outskirts of Kansas City. Inside the office, J.L. filled out the guest register.

"That will be forty-five dollars," the clerk said.

"I'm going to need three extra sheets."

"That will be another twenty dollars," the clerk said.

Once they were inside the motel room, Karina tied a small rope from one light fixture to another between the two beds and hung the sheet, separating the beds.

J.L. inspected it.

"Where did you learn that?"

"During the final days of my divorce, that's the way me and my husband slept."

"You were married?"

"Don't worry about it," she said. "Do you need the bathroom?"

"No," J.L. replied. "Not at the moment."

"I'm going to put on my nightclothes and go to sleep," she

announced. "If you make any move toward me while I'm asleep, I'll scream and the cops will come."

"You don't have to worry," J.L. said. "I have no intention of making moves toward you."

"I'll be up and showered at seven," she said. "I expect to be back on the road by eight. Can we do that?"

"Yes, ma'am," he replied sarcastically. "We can do that."

Going to St. Louis

The next morning, just after 7:00, J.L. was awakened by the sound of the shower running. He sat up in bed and stretched. He heard the bathroom door open slightly.

"I'm coming out," she said. "Are you decent?"

"Give me just a minute," he said.

Quickly, he got out of bed and pulled his clothes on.

"Okay," he said. "Coast is clear."

She came out, freshly showered.

"I'm going to pack my suitcase and I'll meet you at the truck," she instructed.

"Give me about twenty minutes," he replied.

***

An hour later, after a breakfast of scrambled eggs and sausage at the motel's restaurant, they loaded their suitcases, climbed back into J.L.'s truck, and were back on the road. Some twenty minutes out of Kansas City, J.L. turned the truck due east on Interstate 70. As they cruised along the interstate, he could see the rolling plains of central Missouri drifting past.

About an hour later, they passed a stalled car on the side of the highway. About a mile further east, J.L. saw a man in a wheelchair with a gas can.

"In a wheelchair with a gas can?" he asked out loud.

J.L. instinctively started braking the truck and pulled it over to the road shoulder to stop.

"What are you doing?" she asked.

"I'm going to help that guy."

"Oh God, I hope this doesn't end up like the last person you tried to help," she said.

J.L. looked at her.

"I gotta do what I gotta do," he said, bringing the truck to a full stop.

"You're not going to put that poor man up here, are you?"

"I sure am," J.L. replied. "Where else is he going to ride?"

She looked at him disconsolately.

"It won't kill you," J.L. said. "It'll just be for a little while."

She didn't reply.

J.L. got out of the truck and walked back up the highway toward the man. Both of the man's legs had been amputated below the knee. He was patiently rolling the wheelchair with both hands with the gas can hanging on to the side of the wheelchair.

"Hey, partner. Let me help you," J.L. said.

"Thanks, mister," the man replied.

J.L. took the gas can in one hand and pushed the man and the wheelchair to his truck. Then, he opened the passenger door.

"Get out so I can move the ice chest," he ordered.

Karina got out and J.L. moved the ice chest to the back of the truck.

"You sit in the middle," he said to Karina.

She got back in the truck and sat in the middle of the front seat. J.L. physically lifted the man out of the wheelchair into the front seat and put the wheelchair in the back of the truck. He was a short, overweight, round-faced man in his sixties with a bald head.

Five minutes later, the three were cruising eastward.

"Thanks for that," the man said. "That's pretty rough going with that wheelchair in that gravel."

"You're welcome," J.L. said. "Where are you headed?"

"East Tennessee," the man said. "Going to my mother's house at Cumberland Gap."

"There should be an exit up here where we can get some gas," J.L. said.

"The map says about four miles," the man offered.

"We'll get you back on the road here in a few minutes,"

J.L. said.

"My name is Claude," the man said.

"J.L., here."

"Karina," the Latina replied, not looking at the man.

Inside the truck, Karina was very uncomfortable sitting next to the crippled man. She tried to appear to be staring straight ahead at the highway, but out of the corner of her eye, she kept trying to look at the man's amputated stumps.

After a few moments, the man sensed her.

"I see you looking out the corner of your eye like you want to see my stumps," he said. "If you like, I'll show them to you."

"Oh no!" she said guiltily. "That's okay. I don't want to see them."

"Suit yourself," he said.

They rode quietly.

Again, she started glancing out of the corner of her eye to see his stumps.

"Here!" the man said finally. "Let me show you my stumps so you will stop wondering."

He pulled up his trouser legs and revealed the two stumps.

Karina withdrew in muted horror at seeing the stumps.

"It's nothing to be afraid of," he said calmly. "I got them blown off in Vietnam. Stepped on a Viet Cong land mine at Khe Sahn. All I remember was this loud explosion and everything going black. I woke up in the hospital two days later and didn't have any legs. They shipped me from Saigon to San Francisco and I got some artificial legs, but I looked like a spastic on stilts with those things, so I just got a wheelchair."

"That must be terrible," she said.

"Well, you learn to adjust," the man said philosophically. "When life gives you lemons, you make lemonade."

He looked at her.

"If you get my meaning," he said as an afterthought.

"Oh, I get your meaning," she said nervously.

They rode quietly.

Up ahead, J.H. pulled off at the exit and stopped at a service station. Some twenty minutes later, J.L.'s truck had returned to the man's stalled car. J.L. got out and poured the gas into the car's tank. After helping the driver into the passenger seat, he placed the man's wheelchair in the back seat. The man fired up the engine.

"Thank you so much," the man said.

"You're welcome," J.L. replied. "Have a safe trip."

The man waved and J.L. watched as the car sped off up the highway.

J.L. returned to his truck and got in.

"Oh my God, cowboy," she said. "I've never seen anybody without legs before. Oh my God, can you imagine not being able to walk on your own two feet?"

"A man's gotta do what he's got to do in this world," J.L. replied.

She didn't reply.

They rode silently for several minutes.

"That was a wonderful thing you did for that poor man," she said.

J.L. looked at her.

"I try to be a good person," he said. "I believe in karma."

They rode quietly for several minutes.

"Oh, cowboy, I'm so sorry," she said, bursting into tears. "I'm so, so sorry."

"What's wrong?" J.L. asked.

"I'm so sorry," she repeated.

"Sorry for what?"

"For not trusting you," she said, wiping away the tears. "You're really a good person. Please forgive me."

"You're forgiven," J.L. said absently. "Just stop crying, okay?"

She wiped her tears and then blew her nose. They rode quietly.

"Cowboy, I have a confession to make," she said finally.

"Okay," he said nonchalantly. "Let's hear it."

She paused for a moment.

"I'm not really going to St. Louis!" she blurted out.

He looked over at her.

"So where are you going?"

"I'm going to Florida," she said sheepishly.

"To Florida?" he asked in disbelief.

"Yes, Florida," she replied again sheepishly.

He looked at her in disbelief, needing a moment to digest what he had just heard.

"Where are you going in Florida?"

"To Port Everglades," she replied. "It's a little town near Miami."

He looked at her, not really grasping what he was hearing.

"What are you going there for?"

"To take possession of my deceased aunt's estate," she replied.

He smiled and shook his head in disbelief.

"Where are you going?" she asked.

J.L. explained his mission to Miami.

"Looks like we're going to almost the same place," she said.

"Yep, looks that way," J.L. said. "Let's take a look at the map."

Moments later, J.L., pulled the truck to the side of the road, grabbed his map, and got out. Outside, he spread the map on the hood of the truck and, together, they examined the journey. On the highway beside them, cars and trucks whizzed past.

"We'll be in St. Louis tonight," J.L. said thoughtfully, peering closely and tracing their route on the map. "The following night, we'll be in Atlanta and the third night, we should be in Miami."

He turned from the map.

"We should be in Miami in three days," he said resolutely.

"Sounds good to me," she said.

"Then let's do it," J.L. said, starting to fold the map.

She didn't reply.

"Okay?" J.L. asked. "Are you with me?"

She looked at him.

"I have another confession to make," she said.

"Oh God. What is it this time?"

She looked at him apologetically.

"I have eight dollars to my name," she said.

Again, he couldn't believe what he was hearing.

"You mean, you left Oregon and headed to Florida with eight dollars in your pocket?"

"Not exactly," she replied.

"Well, exactly what, then?"

"Well, you see my car broke down in South Dakota and this crazy cowboy stopped to help me—"

She stopped.

"Yes?" he replied.

"I had $675 cash hidden in the glove compartment—"

"And it burned up in the fire?" he said, finishing her statement.

"That's right," she said sheepishly.

He looked at her, shaking his head with annoyance.

"Okay," he said finally. "I've got enough money to get us to Florida, but once we get there, you're on your own."

She looked at him.

"Oh, cowboy!" she said. "Thank you so much!"

She grabbed him, hugged him, and kissed him on the cheek. His black hat was knocked askew.

"Whoa, whoa!" he said, withdrawing from her and straightening his hat. "Now don't you be getting any ideas about me."

She burst out laughing. "Cowboy, you're a weird guy," she said. "I mean, a really weird guy. Okay, I won't be getting any ideas. So we're partners?"

J.L. smiled. "Partners!" he said, offering his hand.

She took his hand and smiled broadly.

"Come on," she said. "Let's go to Florida!"

Friends

An hour later, they were cruising through the open plains of central Missouri.

"My family emigrated from Guatemala to Florida in 1991," she said. "I was eleven. There was me, my parents and three sisters. When we first came to the states, we lived with my Aunt Lydia in Port Everglades until my father could find work.

"Guatemala, huh?" he repeated. "Isn't that one of those little countries around Costa Rica and Nicaragua?"

"No," she replied. "Guatemala is a little further north. It's squeezed in between Mexico, Belize, Honduras, and El Salvador."

"I would have sworn you were Italian with your white skin and jet black hair."

"My father was Spanish," she said, "but my mother was Mexican."

"So how did you get from Florida to the west Coast?"

"I spent three years living with Aunt Lydia in Florida. When I was fourteen, my father got a job in Los Angeles and the family moved to California and settled in San Fernando Valley."

"What town?"

"Reseda," she said. "Me and two of my sisters attended Reseda High during the mid-nineties. I was a bona fide Valley Girl."

J.L. laughed.

"Fer sure! Fer sure!" he joked.

"And from LA to Oregon?"

"In 1998, after I were married, Robert and I lived in the valley for a little over a year, then wandered up to San

Francisco. One day, out of the blue, Robert said he wanted to go to Oregon and join a group of survivalist group..."

"Like a cult?" J.L. interrupted.

"It wasn't really a cult," she said. "The group was called Earth's Blessings, a back-to-the-land group that was basically a commune where everybody worked for the good of everybody else."

"That must have been pretty wild," J.L. said.

"You stayed busy," she said. "There was always something to do. Gardening, mending fences, canning food, cutting hair. That's where I learned to do hair."

They rode quietly. J.L. digested her personal story.

"Why did you get married so young?"

"After I graduated high school, I knew I was going to get away from my father. I wasn't sure how, but I knew I was going to get away. I hated him. I had met Robert at Reseda High. He was from Northern California, played the guitar, had long hair, and loved his freedom. We dated in high school some, but really didn't hit it off. Then one day, after I graduated, I was with some friends in Venice and we met again. We hit it off that time and started dating again. We were married two months later."

"How long were you married?" he asked.

"Eight years," she said. "Two years ago, Robert and I grew weary of the commune and moved to Lake Oswego. That's when our relationship started coming apart. We tried to keep it together but, after a couple years, we both could see it was over. I've been officially divorced for almost two months now."

"Why didn't you tell me the truth about where you were going?" he asked.

"Because I didn't know you and I didn't trust you," she replied. "I didn't want you to know anything about me. I was afraid you would take advantage of me."

He studied her.

"I've always been afraid of men," she added.

"Why?" he asked curiously.

"I'm not sure," she said. "I've asked myself that question many times. I think it goes back to my father."

"Your father?"

"I hated my father," she said. "I hated him for the way he treated my mother. Many nights, he would come home drunk and take out his frustrations on my mother. He would chase her and hit her and hurt her. My other sisters would run from him and say nothing, but I would chase him and kick him for hurting my mother. It went on for years. Some nights, he would come home drunk and my mother would gather up us kids and go stay at a friend's house. The next morning, we would return. He would be sober and go back to work again as if nothing had happened."

J.L. looked at her, saying nothing.

"That's very Freudian," he said.

"Very what?" she asked.

"Very Freudian," he said. "Your explanation follows the teachings of Sigmund Freud."

"If you say so," she said.

They rode quietly as J.L. digested her story.

"Where are your sisters and your mother?"

"Two of my sisters are married with families of their own," she said. "I've got one in New Jersey and one in Minnesota. My youngest sister Luz is somewhere on the road. She's like me, a vagabond at heart."

"And your mother?"

"She still lives in The Valley."

J.L. inhaled.

"So one day you just up and left Lake Oswego out of the blue?"

"No," she replied. "It was time for me to go. My divorce was final. I just wanted to get away. I had too many memories of me and Robert in Lake Oswego. Things we had done, places we had been... There were just too many memories. Most of all, I just wanted to start over. When my aunt's estate was settled two months ago, it was the perfect excuse I needed to get away from Robert and our marriage."

"When did your aunt die?"

"Five months ago," she said. "I didn't go to the funeral. Robert and I couldn't afford it."

Outside the truck, the fallow cornfields, pasturelands, and dense forests of central Missouri rolled past.

"Did you ever make peace with your father?"

She didn't answer. It was as if she had not heard the question.

"Did you ever make peace with your father?" he asked again.

Suddenly, she burst into tears.

He looked at her.

"I didn't mean to make you cry," he said.

"No," she replied. "I want to tell you... Give me just a minute."

She wiped her eyes. She was calmer now.

"When I was growing up, I hated my father so much that I couldn't bear to look at him," she continued. "If we were in the room together, I would never go near him to talk or be close to him. I never sat in my father's lap. I never kissed him or knew the softness of his touch. All the years I was growing up, I never knew who he was or what he was all about because I hated him so much."

J.L. listened silently.

"The only time I was ever near my father during my entire lifetime was after he was dead," she continued. "I went into the funeral home after he died, and I was alone with him for the first time in my life. His face was white, and he was cold to the touch. I looked him full in his face for the first time in my life. I could see his father and his brother in the shape of his head. In his eyes, I could see the Spanish from his father's side of the family. I looked at his hands and they were exactly like mine. Only then did I realize that I had received my hands from my father. We both had long fingers and strong thumbs. For the first time in my whole life, I had some sense of who my father was and what influence he had on my life."

She sniffled, wiped her eyes, and looked out the truck

window.

"What a sad story," he said finally.

"Now you know everything about me," she said. "What about you? Tell me about yourself."

J.L. proceeded to tell the story of his childhood in Oklahoma, his rodeo days, his later years working on ranches and the death of Sara.

"Why did she die so young?" Karina asked.

"She had leukemia," J.L. said. "She was diagnosed one day, and three weeks later, she was dead."

"Sorry to hear that," Karina said. "No children?"

"No," J.L. said. "I had hoped to have a son, but we could never pull off a pregnancy."

A pause.

"Why didn't you have children?" J.L. asked.

"Robert didn't want a child," she said. "He said children were too much trouble. He said he was too selfish to put the time and effort into them they required."

Ahead, J.L. could see a sign: St. Louis City Limits.

"You getting hungry?" he asked.

"Yes," she replied. "I could eat something."

"We'll stop up here on the outskirts of St. Louis," he said. "Mind if I listen to Spanish?"

"No, go ahead," she said.

J.L. loaded the Spanish tape.

"Hablo, hablas, habla, hablamos, habláis, hablas," he repeated.

Karina listened for a moment, the suddenly burst out laughing.

"What's so funny?" he asked.

"Your Southern accent is getting in the way of your Spanish pronunciation."

"So?"

"Spanish is spoken with the tongue against the roof of the mouth," she said. "Look at me!"

She flipped her tongue repeatedly between the roof of her mouth and the back of her teeth and said, "Ta! Ta! Ta! Ta! Ta!

Ta! Ta!"

Finally, she stopped and opened her mouth slightly and showed him how she was placing her tongue against the back of her teeth.

"English is a language that is spoken with the tongue moving all around inside the mouth," she said expertly. "Spanish is spoken with a totally different pattern of tongue movements."

J.L. started trying to click the end of his tongue against the back of his teeth as she had shown him.

"Ta! Ta! Ta! Ta!" he said, trying to imitate the sound she had produced.

Karina laughed politely.

"You need to practice that," she said. "Once you get it down, you'll find it's a lot easier to correctly pronounce Spanish words."

J.L. tried it again.

"Ta! Ta! Ta! Ta! Ta!" he imitated again, clicking the front of his tongue against the back of her upper teeth.

"Say my name," she instructed. "Say Karina."

"Kaw-reeee-nah," J.L. said in his southern drawl.

She laughed.

"That's the first time I ever heard anyone get five syllables out of my name," she said. "Look at my mouth when I say it."

He watched her lip movements.

"Ka-rin-a! Ka-rin-a!" she said. "The sounds are made on the back of the teeth with the tip of the tongue."

J.L. put the tip his tongue on the back of his upper teeth.

"Kaw-ren-a!" he said. "Kaw-ren-a."

"That's better!" she said. "Much better! You just need to practice. You know, there are about ten verbs in Spanish that, if you learn them and their uses, you can say two-thirds of the things you want to say."

"What are the verbs?" he asked.

"Let's stop up here and get some food first," she said. "I'm famished. I'll tell you after we eat."

"Good idea," J.L. said. "I need to stop for gas anyway."

He maneuvered the truck off the main highway and onto a service road.

"Can I ask another question?"

"Sure," she replied.

"Are you afraid of me?"

Startled at the question, she peered at him then burst out laughing.

"No, cowboy," she said finally, trying to control her laughter. "I'm not afraid of you. I was at first, but not anymore. I know now that you're a good person with a kind heart."

"Thanks!" he said.

"You're welcome," she said again with a big smile.

Ralph

Five minutes later, J.L.'s truck pulled into a restaurant on the outskirts of St. Louis. Once they were inside, they could see the place was packed.

"Two?" the waitress asked.

J.L. nodded.

"Right this way, please."

J.L. and Karina followed the waitress.

In the dining area, there were no vacant tables.

"We seem to be full in here," she said. "Would you mind sitting back here with the convention? I mean, if you're real hungry."

"We're real hungry," J.L. said.

With that, the waitress ushered them into a convention area adjacent to the main dining hall where around thirty people sat waiting for a speaker to begin. Plenty of seats were available.

"Is this okay?" she asked.

"This will be fine," J.L. said.

The waitress took their orders.

"Please remain quiet when the speaker begins," she said. "I'll be right back with your orders."

On the podium in front of them, a tall, dark-haired man in his early forties was preparing to speak. Behind him, a large marquee read, "Digital Age Philosophers." The audience fell silent as he motioned for quiet.

"Good afternoon," he began. "My name is Ralph Anderson. As you all know, I am the executive vice president of Digital Age Philosophers. During our last session, Dr. Walter Rothlisberger delivered a lecture on the nature of mechanical media. He explained how, once humankind learned to build fires and melt down hard metals, he created a vast array of mechanical media. This category of media includes everything mechanical—cars, horseshoes, planes, ballpoint pens, plows, bulldozers, tablespoons, bicycles, the space station—anything that involves the melting down and reshaping of hard metals to create practical tools for any purpose."

He motioned into the audience.

"Dr. Rothlisberger, will you please stand up?"

A short, distinguished-looking man wearing a gray beard and glasses stood up in the audience. There was polite applause from the attendees.

"Excellent job, Dr. Rothlisberger," he said. "Now today, I will address the nature of electronic media. First, I want you to meet my wife, Cathy, and my daughter, eleven-year-old Angela," he said, pointing into the crowd. Everyone in the audience, including J.L. and Karina, peered to where he pointed in the audience. A young, dark-haired girl and her mother, who were seated near the speaker's table, waved to the attendees and there was more polite applause.

"Now let's get started with today's session," the speaker said. He started shifting some papers around. At J.L. and Karina's table, their food was being served.

"In the late 19th century, a new category of media—electronic media—appeared," the speaker began. "Inventors like Edison and Alexander Graham Bell and others gave birth to a whole host of new media such as the telegraph, telephone, radio, television, phonograph, and film. These inventions laid the foundation for all other electronic media. By the late 20th century, the computer, the ultimate electronic device, was born...."

Ralph stopped to take a drink of water. He looked down toward his wife and daughter and instantly knew something was wrong.

"Honey," the speaker said, interrupting his speech, "is she all right?"

The mother, an anguished look on her face, was holding

the child by the shoulders.

"I think she's choking," the mother said frantically.

The speaker quickly left the podium and raced down the aisle to his daughter's side. "Yes, she is choking," he announced. "Somebody call 911!" he said frantically. "Call 911! Please, somebody call 911!"

Several people in the audience pulled out their cell phones and started dialing.

"Is there a doctor in the house?" the father pleaded. "Can anyone help?"

Frantically, the father took the child in his arms.

"She's turning blue," the father announced. "She's going to choke to death."

Quickly, J.L. got up and rushed to the father's side.

"Heimlich! Heimlich!" J.L. said.

"What?" the father asked.

"Let me have her," J.L. said confidently.

The helpless father released the child and J.L. stood behind the child and placed his fists at the bottom of her lungs as the father watched. Quickly, he squeezed his fists firmly against the bottom of her ribs. A piece of meat shot out of the girl's mouth and hit her frantic father in the chest. J.L. released the child into her mother's arms as she gasped for breath.

"She'll be okay now," J.L. said.

Suddenly, the child, breathing normally now, was in her mother's arms crying with fright. The agitated father moved to see the child's face. He could see she was breathing normally again. Satisfied his daughter was safe again, he was calmer.

"Oh my God!" he said, turning to J.L. "You saved my daughter's life."

"Somebody had to do something," J.L. replied.

"And you had the presence of mind and self-control to take the necessary action," the father replied. "You're my hero. Thank you so much."

"You're welcome," J.L. said. "It was the right thing to do."

"What's your name?" the speaker asked, offering his hand.

"J.L. Crockett," J.L. replied.

"Pleased to meet you," the speaker said. "I'll always remember you for this."

"It's no big deal," J.L. replied.

"It's a big deal to me," he said. "I love my daughter more than anything else on this earth."

"You're welcome," J.L. said. "How did you ever get a job like this?"

"Oh, this isn't my job," Ralph said. "This is a hobby. I work for the U.S. Park Service."

"Are you a park ranger?"

"Oh no," Ralph said. "I'm in law enforcement. Where are you headed?"

"Miami," J.L. said.

"Really?" Ralph said. "I live in Coral Gables. If you have some time when you're down that way, look me up. I'll have the wife fix a meal. Here's my card."

"Thanks," J.L. replied, taking the card and placing it in his wallet. "That's very hospitable of you. We've got to get back on the road."

"Thanks," Ralph said happily. "I'm not sure how, but some day, some way, I'm going to pay you back for saving my daughter's life."

"I'm sure you will," J.L. replied. "Karma is alive and well."

"Karma is alive and well," Ralph repeated happily. He waved goodbye to J.L. and started back to the podium.

Harold

Late that afternoon, J.L. and Karina crossed the St. Louis county line. Earlier that day, J.L. had told her that he wanted to spend the night in Phillips Crossroads, MO, a little town outside St. Louis, so he could visit Curly's brother, Harold. She had agreed, so about twenty miles west of St. Louis, J.L. turned off the interstate and onto a state road en route to Phillips Crossroads. After some fifteen miles, the four lanes became a two-lane county road and, for a long stretch, all they could see on either side of the highway were forests, mountain ridges, open farmland, and an occasional farmhouse. Darkness was falling.

"Where is this place?" Karina asked impatiently.

"Map says Phillips Crossroads is twenty-two miles south of the interstate," he replied. "Just be patient. We'll be there in a few minutes."

"This place is out in the middle of nowhere," she added.

After another ten miles of more forests and mountain ridges, in the darkness, J.L. saw a sign that read "Phillips Crossroads 12 miles."

"At least we know there is such a place now," she observed.

Finally, they pulled into what was downtown Phillips Crossroads. It was a desolate, rural town with a six-room motel and an attached restaurant. Across the street was a combination garage/service station and what appeared to be a taxi stand.

Twenty minutes later, they had checked into the small hotel. After getting unpacked and getting the privacy sheet in place, they heard a motorcycle pull up in the motel parking lot. J.L. peeked out of the motel window.

"There's Harold," he said.

Karina peeked out the window.

"He looks kind of rough," she said. "Are you sure you trust him?"

"Oh yeah," J.L. said. "He's a good guy. He just likes to project that macho image."

"Everybody is a good guy to you," she said. "I hope you know what you're doing."

"Everything will be fine," J.L. said. "I'll be back in about an hour. I won't be long."

***

Outside, J.L. embraced Harold. Unlike his brother, Harold was a short, stocky man in his early fifties with long, flowing gray hair and a beard. He was wearing motorcycle chains, a denim vest, and motorcycle boots. After greetings, they went into the small restaurant at the motel and ordered food. They talked about the time three years earlier when they had gotten drunk together at the Crazy Horse with Curly and the other Lazy B cowboys. J.L. asked him what kind of work he was doing these days.

"Oh, I've got investments," Harold said.

"What kind of investments?" J.L. asked.

"Oh, you know," Harold said with a nervous laugh, "investment-type investments."

J.L. could see that Harold didn't want to discuss it.

"I'm sure you're doing well," J.L. observed. "Where you living?" he asked.

"I got a cabin up in the hills," Harold replied. "I grow my own vegetables and generate my own electricity. Like you, I love to stay close to the land."

J.L. nodded.

"Well, good for you," J.L. said.

Harold asked about Curly and the Lazy B. J.L. told him that the ranch had been computerized now and the new cowboys on the ranch were computer programmers. J.L. explained that Curly planned on marrying Emily and living happily ever after.

83

Harold laughed.

After another twenty minutes of small talk and reminiscing, they finished their meal and walked back to the motel room.

"Well, it's good to see you," J.L. said.

"Good to see you too," Harold said, shaking his hand and embracing him. "You mind if I use your bathroom?"

"Oh no, that's fine," J.L. said.

With that, J.L. opened the door to the room.

Harold saw Karina, who was sitting at a table looking at the map.

"J.L.," he said, "you didn't tell me you were married."

"She's not my wife," J.L. said. "She's just a friend."

Harold smiled and waved at Karina.

Karina returned the greeting.

"I'll be right out," Harold said, opening the door to the bathroom.

While Harold was in the bathroom, Karina and J.L. spread out a map on a table to discuss their trip. Moments later, Harold exited the bathroom.

"We will be in Memphis tomorrow night and then it's only two more days to Florida," J.L. was explaining to her.

"Okay, old buddy," Harold said. "I'm gone. I'll see you again someday. Not sure when, but I know I'll see you. Pleasure to meet you," he added, waving goodbye to Karina.

Moments later, they heard the motorcycle fire up and then pull away from the hotel.

"I don't trust that guy," she said.

"You worry too much," J.L. said. "Come on; let's get some rest. I want to get on the road early tomorrow."

***

The following morning, J.L. was awakened by the sound of the shower. He sat up in bed, stretched, and looked at the clock. It was 7:30. He was right on schedule.

He heard the bathroom door open.

"Are you decent?" she asked.

"No, but I will be in a minute," he said.

84

Moments later, he was out of bed, had his clothes on, and, after she emerged from the bathroom, went in for his shower.

Once he had showered, he put on his clothes for the new day and found his wallet and loose change, but no truck keys. He looked on the dresser, in his previous day's pants, and on the floor. No truck keys.

"Did you do something with the truck keys?" he asked as she was packing her suitcase.

"No." she said. "Why?"

He stopped and rushed to the window and quickly drew back the curtain.

"My truck!" he said. "My truck is gone!"

He opened the door and looked out.

"Son-of-a bitch!" he shouted. "Son of a bitch! That goddamn Harold stole my truck. He lifted the keys when I let him go in to use the bathroom."

He took off his hat and slapped it against his thigh in anger.

"And he got my new ice chest!" he shouted. "Son of a goddamn bitch!"

"And he got my cell phone," she added angrily. "I left it in there charging."

For a moment, J.L. waited for the realization to sink in.

J.L. looked at her. She was showered, her suitcase was packed, and she was ready to go.

"I guess we'll have to report it to the police," she said.

J.L. packed his suitcase, went to the front office, and asked the clerk to call the police. Thirty minutes later, a fat county police officer arrived and J.L. explained what happened.

"You think this guy Harold Watson stole your truck?" the cop asked.

"Yeah," J.L. said. "I'm absolutely sure. He got the keys when we went into the room after dinner."

J.L. explained that he knew Harold through his brother Curly.

"You got a description?"

.J.L. described Harold as best he could as the cop took

notes. He asked J.L. what other information he had about Harold and whether he had any identifying marks. J.L. answered as best he could. Some fifteen minutes later, the officer had prepared a report.

"We'll do what we can," the officer said, handing J.L. the report, "but I have to tell you we don't find stolen vehicles around here very often. Usually stolen vehicles get taken to chop shops, get tore down for their parts, and end up in Chicago and places further north. Maybe this report will help you get your money from the insurance company."

"That's just great," J.L. said sarcastically, snatching the report from the officer's hand.

"I'm sorry," the officer said. "There's nothing else I can do for you."

J.L., fuming with anger, didn't reply.

"Have a good day," the officer said with finality and turned and walked back to his patrol car.

J.L. and Karina, suitcases in hand, watched silently as the county patrol car pulled out of the motel parking lot and disappeared in a cloud of dust down the highway.

"Son of a bitch! Son of a bitch!" J.L. shouted. "Goddamn son of a bitch!"

He paused for a moment.

"Son of a bitch!" he shouted angrily, kicking his suitcase with all of his might. "Son of a bitch! Son of a bitch! Son of a bitch!"

He stopped. He was out of breath.

All this time, she had been watching him.

"For such a peaceful man, you can get pretty violent."

He didn't reply.

"Who are you mad at?" she asked.

"Myself, more than anybody else," he said. "I'm such a fricking naïve idiot."

"Yep!" she said matter-of-factly. "He stole that truck right out from under your nose. Like a lamb to slaughter."

J.L. didn't reply.

"Okay," he said. "I guess I deserved that one."

"So what do we do now?" she asked.

"What do you mean by 'what do we do now'?"

"We're still partners, aren't we?" she asked.

J.L. inhaled and looked at her.

"Yeah," he replied with some hesitation. "We're still partners."

Calmer now, he looked across the street to the service station garage.

"Come on," he said.

Insurance Salesman

Across the street, J.L. and Karina, suitcases in hand, approached the service station/garage. Behind the counter, they saw a fat teenager sipping a soda and watching a television show. "You got any taxis going down to St. Louis?" J.L. asked. "Do you see any taxis around here?" the teenager replied, obviously annoyed that he was being distracted from the TV show.

"Sign out front says 'taxis,'" J.L. replied

"That sign has been out there for years," the teenager replied.

"Any way to get a ride to St. Louis?"

"Go next door and talk to Wallace," the teenager said. "He might have something."

J.L. turned to go.

"Hey, mister!" the fat teenager called.

"Are you a real cowboy?"

"No, I'm a figment of your imagination," J.L. said.

"A what?" the teenager asked with a puzzled look.

"I didn't really come in here today," J.L. said sarcastically. "You're looking at a ghost."

The fat teenager was at a loss for words.

"You don't have to get huffy," he said finally. "I just thought I would ask."

J.L. turned and he and Karina left the taxi stand and approached the garage next door. They didn't see anybody inside.

"Hello," J.L. said.

No answer.

Then J.L. saw a pair of legs sticking out from under a car.

"Hello," J.L. called again, louder this time.

Moments later, a short, stocky man rolled out from under the car. He was flat on his back on a mechanic's creeper. He wore greasy clothing and his face had smudges of black grease here and there.

"Excuse me," J.L. asked. "Can you tell me where Wallace is?"

"I'm Wallace," he said, getting up from the creeper. "What can I do for you?"

"We're looking for transportation down to St. Louis."

"I don't have anything," he said.

"Nothing?" J.L. asked.

Wallace shook his head.

"We're desperate," J.L. said.

The man studied J.L. for a moment.

"Well, in that case—"

He stopped.

"Come out back with me," he continued.

J.L. and Karina followed the man to the back of the garage. The man stopped in front of an old bicycle.

"I got this old bicycle here," he said. "My son left it before he started driving a big rig."

"Is that all you got?" J.L. asked.

"'Fraid so," the man said.

J.L. sat down his suitcase and inspected the bicycle.

"That back tire needs some air in it," he said.

"I'll pump it up," the man said.

"How much?"

"I'll take thirty dollars."

"Give you twenty dollars."

"Sold," Wallace said.

Moments later, they were inside the garage and the man was pumping up the front tire. Once inflated, J.L. tested it.

"Should be okay now," J.L. said, handing the man twenty dollars.

"Thank you!" Wallace said, taking the money. "It's eight miles down that mountain to St. Louis."

With that, J.L. rolled the bicycle out of the garage to the

side of the highway. Then, he turned to Karina.

"Let's go," he said.

She looked at him incredulously.

"Are you serious?"

"You want to walk to St. Louis?" he asked.

"You mean you want me to get on that thing and actually ride it?"

"That's the idea," J.L. said impatiently.

She sighed and shook her head.

***

Twenty minutes later, J.L. and Karina were riding the bicycle down the mountainside. J.L. was pedaling and Karina was seated on the crossbar with their suitcases securely tied over the rear tire.

"I hope that front tire holds up," J.L. said.

They were on a steep mountain grade and J.L. had taken his feet off the pedals and was letting the bike coast downhill. The bike was traveling fast down the steep mountainside.

"Slow this thing down," she yelled. "You're going to get us killed."

"The faster we go, the faster we'll get to St. Louis," he said.

Suddenly, there was a loud pop. J.L. tried to guide the bicycle off the highway, but once he hit the loose gravel along the side of the road, he lost control, and the two of them and the bicycle veered erratically off the road and crashed down an embankment.

"Yaaaiiiii," Karina screamed as the bicycle crashed down the embankment.

Moments later, J.L. found himself sprawled in a bush. Nearby, he could see Karina raising herself to her elbows. He stood up and started dusting himself off.

"Cowboy!" she screamed, looking up at him. "I told you that you were going too fast! Don't you ever listen?"

She got up angrily and dusted off her clothes. They looked over at the bicycle. It was a twisted heap of useless metal. As J.L. started to remove the suitcases from the wrecked bicycle,

90

they heard a car screech to a halt on the road above them.

A tall, balding man in his early forties, wearing glasses and a pocket protector, peered down at them.

"Are you people hurt?" he asked, surveying the scene. "Do you have insurance? You know, I could write you a bicycle policy. It would cost each of you thirty-eight dollars a year. Got the papers in the car."

"Insurance is the last thing on our minds right now," J.L. said, helping Karina to her feet.

"Are you okay?" he asked.

"I'm okay," she replied, dusting herself off and picking up her suitcase.

The man peered at the bicycle.

"Looks like that bicycle ain't going nowhere," the man said. "I can take you down to St. Louie if you like."

"We'd appreciate that," J.L. said.

***

Ten minutes later, J.L. and Karina were in the back of the man's car, speeding down the mountainside toward St. Louis.

"Williard is the name and insurance is the game," he said. "You know, if you need insurance, I got it all. I can insure you for fire, flood, theft, health, auto, dental, vision, chiropractic, guaranteed issuance, alternative therapy, burial, single indemnity, double indemnity, triple indemnity—I tell you, I got insurance. I can insure your ma, your pa, your dog, your cow, your tractor—I'm telling you, I can even insure you against your insurance company. In other words, if you file a claim and your insurance company doesn't pay, this policy will cover what the insurance company owes you."

The man grew silent.

"I really don't think we're interested," J.L. said.

"Cowboy, let me ask you something," the man said. "When you're out on the range and roping little doggies, don't you ever fall off the horse and break an arm or a leg or get a concussion? In the springtime, when you're branding calves, do you ever burn yourself? Your hand or your arm? You know those branding irons must get pretty hot. I can write you

91

policies for those things."

"Cowboys don't rope doggies and brand calves anymore," J.L. replied. "Computers do those things these days."

"What?" the man exclaimed. "You're pulling my leg."

"Nope," J.L. said. "Computers have put cowboys out of business."

The man turned to Karina.

"What about you?" he asked. "Do you need insurance? I can insure you against breast cancer, diabetes, miscarriages, vaginitis, mastitis, shingles, amenorrhea, leucorrhea, and biofiliosis."

"What's biofiliosis?" she asked.

"Biofiliosis is an obscure woman's ailment in which the lining of the uterus becomes infected with a parasite known as McDermott's elongated hookworm. I once sold a woman in Chicago three policies. Her sister and her mother died of biofiliosis. She bought one for herself and two for her dogs."

"Her dogs?" Karina asked.

"Yep," the insurance salesman replied proudly. "Although there has never been a known case of biofiliosis in dogs, she just wanted to be sure they were covered."

"No," Karina said. "I don't think I need any of those."

They rode quietly for a few minutes.

Finally, Williard turned to J.L.

"Where you from?" he asked.

"Texas, originally," J.L. said.

"I was in Texas one time selling cobra insurance," the man said.

"There are no cobras in Texas," J.L. said.

"Yeah, but I didn't tell anybody that," he said with an air of satisfaction. "I sold thirteen policies. One guy tried to collect and, during the trial, he died from a rattlesnake bite en route to the courthouse. Before he died, he said he wished he had bought rattlesnake insurance instead."

They rode quietly.

"Look!" J.L. said, pointing ahead. "There's the St. Louis Arch."

Karina peered into the direction he was pointing.

"Yeah," she said. "I see it."

"I think we'll get out here," J.L. said.

"Why?" Williard asked. "I was just starting to enjoy your company."

"I want to walk under the arch," J.L. said.

"Okay, I understand," Williard said. "Are you sure you don't need any insurance?"

"We're sure," J.L. said.

With that, J.L. and Karina, suitcases in hand, got out of the car and started walking up the service road.

"Let's go down here and see if we can find a bank," he said.

"I thought you wanted to walk under the arch," she said.

"No," he replied. "I just wanted to get away from that guy. He was really getting on my nerves."

Crossing the Mississippi

J.L. and Karina started walking along the sidewalk of the service road.

After they had walked several blocks, J.L. saw a homeless man standing on the corner, probing through a garbage can.

"Excuse me," J.L. said. "Do you know where there's a bank around here?"

The homeless man looked at him.

"If you'll give me fifty cents for a bottle, I'll tell you," the man said.

"Oh, what the hell," J.L. said, reaching in his pocket and handing the man said change.

The homeless man counted.

"There's only forty-seven cents here," he said.

J.L. reached in his pocket again and handed the man more change.

Satisfied with his pay, the homeless man turned and pointed up the street.

"See the red light?" the man said. "That's Lewis and Clark. Follow Lewis and Clark for three blocks and you'll see a bank on the right side. It's Missouri Federal or something like that."

***

Fifteen minutes later, J.L. and Karina were at the teller's counter in the Missouri Federal bank.

"I want to withdraw some money on a credit card," J.L. said.

"Our computers are down right now," the teller said. "It may take a while."

"How long?" J.L. asked.

"Let me ask," the teller replied.

She turned to a nerdy-looking young man wearing thick glasses who had his head stuck into a bank of computers.

"How long before the computers are fixed?" she asked.

"It all depends," he said. "It looks like the firmware is not loading properly into the appropriate memory segments," he said. "If I don't have to replace any memory chips and we can get the mirrored terabyte hard drives to come up cleanly, it might be ten to fifteen minutes. On the other hand, if we have to run the Super Solve software again on the LLT, provided we have enough RAM, then the BIOS should load much faster and we won't have it up for another hour or more."

The teller turned to J.L.

"Did you get that?" she asked.

J.L. nodded and then glanced over to the wall socket.

"Do you think it would help if you plugged it in?" J.L. asked.

"Oh!" said the computer guy, noticing there was no power. He plugged the cord in and the bank of computers made a series of digital sounds and the lights went up.

"Can I have your card?" the teller asked.

J.L. handed her the card and she swiped it through the reader. Then, she passed the portable device to him and asked him to enter his PIN.

J.L. punched in his PIN and the lights in the bank dimmed, flicked several times, and all of the electrical power in the bank went off. The only light coming into the bank was the sunlight streaming through the bank's glass front door.

The computer guy stepped forward.

"I was afraid that would happen," he said. "The DBT data load on the distribution magnifier was not sufficiently coordinated with the RSP. We won't have this box fixed until sometime tomorrow."

J.L. looked disgustedly at Karina.

"Come on," he said.

Outside the bank, they started walking up the street. Suddenly, J.L.'s ears perked up. "I hear a train," he said. "It sounds like it's over here. Come on!"

J.L. and Karina followed the sound for about a block to a set of railroad tracks. There, in the distance, they could see a train disappearing.

"What were you going to do?" she asked.

"I used to hop trains when I was a teenager in Oklahoma," he said. "It's a very cheap form of transportation."

"Hop a train?" she said curiously. "You mean jump on a train and ride it like they do in the movies?"

He nodded.

"Are you crazy?" she asked incredulously. "Do you have any idea of how many people have been killed doing that?

"Do you want to get to Florida?" he asked.

She sighed and said nothing.

They walked along the track for about fifteen minutes, suitcases in hand, stepping from tie to tie.

"After all," he said, finally, "it's a beautiful day for a walk. The sun is shining, the birds are singing—"

J.L. stopped and cupped his ear facetiously as if he were listening for a bird. In the distance, a bird sang.

"Hear that Jo-Ree?" he said.

She looked at him and shook her head disapprovingly.

"You're nuts," she said. "Absolutely crazy!"

"You worry too much," he said. "Karma has a way of taking care of its own."

Suddenly, they heard a loud, squealing sound like raw metal being grated against raw metal. They turned to the direction of the sound. Coming around the curve on the track, they saw a handcar slowly winding its way toward them. Pumping the handcar was an old black man with a headful of white hair and dressed in a white tee shirt and faded overalls, staring straight ahead. As the handcart neared them, they saw that his eyes were milky white without pupils and he was blind.

"I am yo karma," the old black man said as the handcart drew closer. "Wherever you go, I go. Wherever I go, you go. Though my eyes are blind, I see all the world."

The handcar stopped in front of them. "You white folks going down the river?" the old black man asked.

"Yeah," J.L. replied. "How did you know?"

"Get on," the old black man said.

"Gee, thanks," J.L. said. "That's very nice of you."

J.L. and Karina took a seat on the handcar.

Once J.L. and Karina were comfortably seated, the old black man started to pump again and the handcar started moving slowly down the track

"See," J.L. said. "I told you. You worry too much."

"You don't think he's going to rob us or throw us in the river, do you?"

"Are you crazy?" he asked. "He's just an old black man. And he's blind. How can he hurt us?"

"Last time you said that, we lost the truck," Karina said. "And my cell phone."

"Will you let that rest for a while?" he said with obvious annoyance.

They grew quiet. The only sound was the creaking metal on metal sound of the old black man pumping the handcar.

"Though my eyes are blind, I see all the world," he said prophetically. "Here I see need and bleed and weed. Here I see dogs and bogs and logs and a big bumblebee pulling y'all up into its belly. And then I see love... Oh, great Lord above."

With that, the handcar slowed to a stop.

They were on the east bank of the Mississippi River.

"See that little path down there among those red oak saplings?" the old black man said.

J.L. peered to where he was pointing and then he turned back.

"I thought you were blind?" J.L. said.

"Listen to me," the old black man said.

"Yeah," J.L. said, "I see the path."

"Y'all go on down there," the old black man said. "There's a crazy white boy down there that will take y'all down the river."

"How do you know that?" J.L. asked curiously.

"Just do as I say," the old black man replied.

J.L. shrugged and they got off the handcar.

"Thanks for the ride," J.L. said.

"Thanks," Karina said, waving goodbye.

The old black man, still staring straight ahead, started pumping the handcar again.

"I am yo karma," he said, as the handcart started slowly moving down the tracks again in a chorus of loud squeals. "Wherever you go, I go. Wherever I go, you go. Though my eyes are blind, I see all the world."

Karina looked at J.L.

"That was weird," she said. "What do you think he meant about dogs and bogs and logs?"

"Who knows?" J.L. said disinterestedly. "He's just an old man. Come on."

The Commodore

Together, suitcases in hand, J.L. and Karina started down the path from the railroad tracks to the banks of the Mississippi River. It was a steep, downhill dirt path lined on either side with a mixture of red oaks, sweet gum, and hickory saplings. After they had scrambled halfway down the path, J.L. heard a voice and stopped. Karina stopped behind him. J.L. peered through the trees toward the riverbank. Docked on the river, bobbing quietly in the muddy water, J.L. could see a white river boat, maybe forty feet long, with several cabins. On the upper deck, he saw a pilot's station with a steering helm and a bank of navigation devices. On the lower deck, he spotted a tall young man in his late twenties, with long, dark hair, thick glasses, and wearing a white captain's cap. He was pacing back and forth across the deck, talking to himself. J.L. and Karina listened.

"So if Colonel Jefferson and the Confederate Queen went down at the lowest point south of St. Louis, it would have to have been just north of the third big sandbar at Memphis. That's the only place it could be."

"Hello!" J.L. called.

The young man, oblivious to his surroundings, continued talking and pacing.

"That means, at low tide, the remains of the *Confederate Queen* would have to be sitting just north of the third sandbar."

"Hello!" J.L. called again, louder this time.

The young man stopped pacing and peered through the thicket toward J.L.

"Hello," the young man answered.

"I understand you're going down to Memphis," J.L.

offered.

"Yes, tonight," the young man replied. "Why do you ask?"

"We need a ride."

"Can you work for your passage?"

"Yes," J.L. replied.

"Y'all come on down," the young man said.

Moments later, J.L. and Karina walked across the dock to the boarding entrance on the boat. As they approached, the young man unfastened a rope barrier between the dock and the boat.

"Welcome aboard," he said stiffly.

"My name is J.L. Crockett," J.L. said, offering his hand.

The young man instantly sprang to attention and saluted J.L and Karina in Navy style.

"Commodore William James Perry at your service, sir," he said, holding the military-style pose and not shaking J.L.'s hand.

"Pleased to meet you," J.L. said.

"This is your wife?" the young man asked, indicating Karina.

"No," J.L. replied. "She's just a friend. This is Karina."

Once again, the young man sprang to attention and saluted her. Karina acknowledged the greeting.

"What sort of work did you want me to do?" J.L. asked.

"I'm looking for the remains of the *Confederate Queen*," the young man said. "It was a Confederate States commercial trading ship that went down in this river in 1854. My research indicates that it went down just north of Memphis. I've been in St. Louis for almost two months researching it. There was almost a million dollars in gold bullion on that ship headed for a Confederate bank in Alabama. It was never recovered. I plan to find it and claim it."

"So what do you want me to do?" J.L. asked again.

"Well, I've got this underwater sonar device here," he said, pointing to a square, waist-high piece of equipment on the back of the boat. "That sonar will pick up the wreckage of the Confederate Queen if it's where I think it is. We might even find the chests of gold bullion near the wreckage. At low tide tomorrow morning, I plan on finding that shipwreck and seeing what's down there. I need someone to steer the boat while I'm probing the bottom. Ever had any river pilot experience?"

"When I was teenager, I spent a couple summers on shrimp boats out of Galveston, but I've never actually piloted one," J.L. said.

"It's not that hard," the younger man said. "You can drive a car, can't you?"

"Yes," J.L. said, "but I don't have a license for one of these."

"You don't need one," the commodore replied. "I'm a licensed river pilot. I'll swear you in as my first mate and we'll be in business."

"Well," J.L. said, "I guess there's a first time for everything."

"Hold up your right hand," the commodore ordered.

Karina watched curiously as J.L. held up his right hand.

"Do you, J.L. Crockett, being of sound mind and body, and recognizing the dangers that lie before you, swear to obey all of the laws of the U.S. Maritime Commission as well as faithfully carry out all of the orders of your captain, Commodore William James Perry?"

"I do," J.L. said.

"Good," the commodore replied. "Now let's look at the map."

The commodore unfolded a map and placed it on top of the sonar device on the stern of the boat.

"Right here," he said, indicating on the map, "is where the *Queen* went down. It's about a quarter mile north of Memphis. Parts of the wreckage as well as identifiable relics from the ship have washed ashore on the river's east bank. At low tide tomorrow, I want to start probing the bottom with the sonar while you steer the boat. I'll take her downriver tonight and I'll awaken you at 0600 hours tomorrow to begin the search. That way, you and your wife can get some rest tonight."

"She's not my wife," J.L. said.

"Well, whatever she is," the commodore replied disinterestedly. "Go to your quarters. Third cabin on the right. You'll find peanut butter and jelly sandwiches in the refrigerator in the galley."

"Peanut butter and jelly sandwiches?" J.L. asked.

"Yes," the commodore replied. "Peanut butter and jelly sandwiches. We run a tight ship here. Now go to your quarters, sailor. You will be awakened for duty call immediately at 0600 hours."

"Aye, aye, sir," J.L. said, saluting obediently.

***

Moments later, J.L. and Karina opened the door to the designated cabin. Inside, they saw two bunks with a small sitting area and a desk. They went inside.

Karina threw her suitcase on the bed and burst out laughing.

"Aye, aye, sir," she said, standing at attention and mocking J.L.'s salute. Then, she fell back on the bed in uncontrollable laughter. Finally, she stopped laughing. "I'll tell you, cowboy," she said. "You take the cake."

"A man's got to do what he's got to do in this world," J.L. said.

"You talk about a lunatic," she said. "I'm telling you, this guy is not playing with a full deck."

"You can laugh and make fun all you want to," J.L. said. "If he gets us down to Memphis tomorrow, I'll play his little sailor game as long as he likes."

"You don't realize how dangerous this guy is," she said. "If we get killed in this thing, it's going to be your fault."

"You worry too much," he replied. "You're always afraid the world is out to get you."

"I haven't had any trucks stolen from me lately," she replied.

J.L. looked at her, an annoyed expression on his face.

"Will you lay off of me for a while?" he said. "Look, I'm just trying to fulfill my end of the deal."

"Yeah, you're right," she said, calmer now. "I understand. I just got a little carried away."

"Come on," J.L. said. "Let's get some rest."

"I'm not unpacking my suitcase," she said.

"Neither am I," he replied. "I'm going to be ready for anything with this guy."

***

Promptly at 6:00 the next morning, the commodore awoke J.L. from a deep sleep. When he sat up in bed and rubbed his eyes, he could see first light out of the cabin window. Moments later, J.L. was at the helm of the boat, taking instructions from the commodore.

"We'll see the seafood restaurant on the east bank of the river," the commodore said. "At that point, the third sandbar will be another fifty to sixty yards down river along the east bank. I want you to take her close to shore and hold her steady while I probe. You got that?"

"Got it," J.L. said.

"Okay," the commodore said. "Let's get started."

As J.L. navigated the boat along the river between the other boats, he started to enjoy himself. He remembered his teenage days he had spent in the Gulf of Mexico with shrimpers and recalled his boyhood dreams of perhaps being a shrimper himself someday. He was having fun.

For about thirty minutes, J.L. navigated the boat down the river.

"There's the seafood restaurant," the commodore said. "Take her about thirty yards offshore and I'll start probing."

As instructed, J.L. turned the boat toward the east shore until it was some thirty yards out.

"Steady as she goes," the commodore instructed, peering into the screen of the sonar device and watching the scanning beam circle the screen.

"Hold her steady," the commodore ordered.

"I'm holding," J.L. replied, pulling back gently on the throttle.

The commodore peered into the sonar device.

"There it is! There it is!" he yelled excitedly. "Take her a little to the right."

J.L. turned the helm slightly right.

"Too much! Too much!" the commodore shouted. "Go left! Left!"

J.L. followed the instructions.

"Hard left! Hard left!!" the commodore shouted.

J.L. turned the wheel as far as he could.

"It won't go any further left," he shouted back.

"Force it! Force it!" the commodore yelled. "Jerk the wheel to the left."

"I'm afraid I'll break something," J.L. replied.

"Jerk it!" the commodore ordered. "Jerk it!"

With all his strength, J.L. jerked the helm to the left.

As he did, he felt a steering cable snap. He spun the helm to the right, and then the left, but the vessel failed to respond. He no longer had control of the boat. The vessel lurched sideways out of control and was at the mercy of the river's current.

"We have no steering!" J.L. shouted.

"Jesus Christ!" the commodore shouted, looking up at J.L. "What did you do?"

J.L. left the helm and rushed to the cabin as the boat was swept aimlessly downstream. He rushed into the cabin. Karina was still asleep.

"Wake up! Wake up!" he shouted. "We're getting off this tub!"

"What?" she said, sitting up and rubbing her eyes.

"There's no steering. This thing is going to crash!" he shouted. "Come on! Grab your suitcase! We've got to hurry!"

Now wide-awake, she grabbed her suitcase. J.L. hastily threw items in his suitcase and they darted out the cabin door.

Moments later, suitcases in hand, they were standing on the deck. As they stood on the deck facing the river's east bank, J.L. could see a boat dock coming up about forty yards ahead. J.L. took off his black hat and tucked it inside his belt.

"Okay," he said. "Get ready to jump."

"We're going to jump?" Karina asked, realizing what was happening.

"We can't stay on this thing," J.L. said.

"I can't swim," she said frantically.

"That's okay," he replied calmly. "We can use our suitcases for flotation. If you go under when we jump, hold your breath! I'll hold your hand and we'll come up together."

"Oh God!" she said nervously. "Oh God! Oh God!"

J.L. watched and waited as the boat neared the wooden pier.

"Get ready," J.L. said, taking her hand into his. "I'll tell you when."

She grasped his hand tightly.

"One—two—three—jump!" J.L. commanded.

Memphis

Together, hand in hand, they jumped into the muddy water. For a moment, they disappeared under the surface. J.L.'s hatless head bobbed to the surface first. A second later, Karina's head shot to the surface. She was coughing and spitting out water. He was still holding her hand.

"Are you okay?" he asked.

"Oh God! I think so," she replied, still spitting out water.

"I'm going to release your hand now," he said. "Put that hand on my suitcase and I'll paddle us to shore."

She did as instructed.

Moments later, J.L. and Karina were standing safely on the east shore of the river. Both were soaking wet. J.L. pulled his black hat out of his waistband. As he did, water poured out. He fluffed it out to its original form as best he could. Then, he turned to her.

"Come on," he said. "Let's go up here and see what we can find."

Suitcases in hand, they started up the river's east bank squishing and squashing in their wet clothes. They heard a young man's shouting voice downriver.

"Abandon ship! Every man for himself! Repel boarders! Damn the torpedoes, full steam ahead! Arrivederci, Roma!"

J.L. looked at Karina.

"That would be the commodore," he said.

Karina nodded her agreement and they continued squishing and squashing up the river's bank. As they approached the top of the bank, they saw an old woman sitting in a rocking chair reading the Bible. She had long, gray hair, looked to be in her late seventies, and was wearing an apron.

On one side of the rocker, there was a foot tub half-full of unpeeled apples. Beside the foot tub sat a bowl of freshly peeled apples. She looked up from the Bible.

"Well, bless Pat," she said upon seeing them. "Look at what that river brought me today."

"Howdy, ma'am!" J.L. said sheepishly, removing his soaking wet hat.

"What in God's name are you two kids doing coming out of that river like a couple of river rats?"

"Well, we were on a river boat that was about to crash," J.L. offered.

"I ain't got time to listen to no foolishness," she interrupted. She stopped when the three of them heard a loud crashing sound downriver. She peered downriver toward the sound.

"That's the boat we were on," J.L. said.

"Well, whatever," she said disinterestedly. "Y'all come on up to the house; I'll get y'all all dried and fed."

With that, she tucked the bowl of quartered apples in her apron, picked up the foot tub with the unpeeled apples, and started to the nearby house. She stopped and turned to J.L.

"Would you mind bringing my Bible and dipping snuff?" she asked. "The snuff is under the rocker."

"Be happy to," J.L. said.

An hour later, they were sitting at the old woman's table eating fried catfish, mashed potatoes, black-eyed peas, and cornbread with iced tea. Virtually everything in the room, as well as the rest of the house, had a religious connotation. On the wall beside the table, there was a huge portrait of a sorrowful Christ, hands bleeding and crowned with thorns, languishing on the cross. There were several smaller engraved religious plaques scattered throughout the room. One read: The Way of the Cross Leads Home. Another said: Give me my flowers while I live. Still another proclaimed: Jesus loves you! Also, there were several well-worn Bibles scattered around the house. She said her name was Rhoda.

"This is really good," J.L. said, wolfing down a bite of

fried catfish. "I hadn't had any southern cooking since I left Texas."

"Thanks for helping us," Karina said, helping herself to more catfish.

"Be not forgetful to entertain strangers for some have entertained angels unaware. Hebrews 13:2," the old woman quoted.

She turned to J.L.

"J.L., are you a religious person?" she asked.

"They tried to baptize me when I was ten years old in Texas, but it didn't take," he replied.

"Didn't take?" she asked.

"I mean, it wasn't in my heart," he replied. "I only did it because my mother wanted me to be baptized."

"I'm the kind of person that always needed religion," she replied. "About all I ever had in my life was my faith and my brother Horace. I never had no luck with men and Horace never had no luck with women. So, after our parents died, we lived together in this house for thirty-two years. He worked at the linoleum factory over in town and I took care of the house. After he died in 2005, I've lived here alone. You know, them's a dead man's clothes you're wearing," she said. "Horace wore those before he went to heaven."

"Oh, I wear dead men's clothes every day," J.L. said with a smile. "At least they're dry."

"I always looked forward to going to church," she continued. "It gave me a peace and a solace I couldn't find anywhere else. It gave me hope for my life and allowed me to find happiness inside myself. I feel that, when I die, I will go to Heaven and Jesus will welcome me into his arms. And I know my Bible. I could have been a preacher, but most folks don't take kindly to women preaching the gospel, especially southern folks."

"Good for you," J.L. said. "I'm happy that you have found something that allows you to be still within yourself. The greatest gift that life has to offer is peace of mind."

"Would you like some more biscuits?" she asked.

"No, I'm finished," J.L. said. "You're such a good cook." She got up and started cleaning the table.

"Let me check the dryer," she said. "I should have some dry, clean clothes for y'all now."

She disappeared into another room for several minutes and then reappeared with a stack of freshly cleaned clothes for J.L and Karina.

"Okay," she said with an air of finality, "I've got you kids fed and dried out. I've got to peel the rest of them apples."

"Yes, ma'am, and we've got to be moving on ourselves," J.L. said.

***

Ten minutes later, J.L. and Karina, suitcases in hand, and the old woman were standing in the front yard of her home saying their goodbyes.

"Before you go, I want you to take these with you," the old woman said. "Here are two slabs of sweet potato pie. You can eat these on your journey."

"Thank you very much," J.L. said.

Karina took the two slabs of pie, opened her suitcase, and placed them safely inside.

"For I was hungry and you fed me. I was thirsty and you gave me drink. Matthew 25:31," the old woman quoted.

"Can you tell us where there's a bank?" J.L. asked.

"Yes, go down to Front Street and follow it until you reach Beale. Go left on Beale Street; you'll see the bank on the right."

"Thanks for helping us," Karina called and she and J.L. waved goodbye and started walking up the street.

"Do not neglect to do good and to share what you have with others, for such sacrifices are pleasing to God. Hebrews 13:16," she quoted and waved goodbye for the last time.

"Remember," she called after them, "left on Beale Street."

Ghost

Twenty minutes later, J.L. and Karina were standing at the teller's window in a bank on Beale Street. The teller swiped J.L.'s credit card and said, "Enter your password."

J.L. punched his pin into the machine.

"It's being rejected," she said.

"Let me try it again," he said.

The teller swiped the card again.

J.L. entered the pin again.

"I'm sorry," the teller said, "your password is being rejected."

"Okay, okay," J.L. said disgustedly. "Let me have it back."

J.L. took the credit card, and he and Karina turned and started out of the bank.

As they passed the line of waiting customers, they heard a woman's voice call out. J.L. stopped and turned to the direction of the voice. There stood an older woman, early fifties with an expensive look and a shock of red hair. She was staring intently at J.L.

"Excuse me," she said.

"Is something wrong?" J.L. asked.

"Isn't your name J.T. or J.R. or something like that?" she asked tentatively.

"J.L." he replied.

"And you used to ride the rodeo?" she asked.

J.L. nodded.

The red-haired woman smiled.

"You don't remember me, do you?"

"No, ma'am, I don't," J.L. said, shaking his head.

"I'm Norma Jac Shoulders," she replied. "I'm Bill

Shoulders' older sister. I met you in Oklahoma City one time."

J.L. burst out laughing.

"Oh yes," he replied. "I remember now. That was a long time ago."

"Twelve years," she said. "What are you doing here in Memphis?"

J.L. explained their dilemma.

"Well, maybe I can help you some," she said. "Atlanta is one of your stops. Right?"

J.L. nodded.

"Soon as I'm finished here, I'm going back there," she said. "If you like, y'all can ride with me. I'd love to talk to you and catch up."

"Sure," J.L. said. "We'd appreciate that."

***

Thirty minutes later, they were cruising southeast on Highway 78 toward Birmingham. Karina and Norma Jac sat in the front seat while J.L was in the back. Norma Jac and Karina were chitchatting and getting along quite well.

"You grew up in Guatemala?" Norma Jac was asking. "Guatemala City?"

"Oh no," Karina said. "Tilapa. Do you know Guatemala?"

"I was in Guatemala City for a week one time," she recalled. "When I was going to the University of Georgia and studying languages, I spent a summer touring Mexico and Central America. Honey, that was before you were even born."

"Did you like Guatemala?"

"Yes," she said. "It was a very clean country. People were very nice, but very religious. Oh my goodness, they were so poor. You know, Americans who have everything in the world at their fingertips notice those things right away."

"Yes, we were very poor when I was growing up," Karina said. "My father worked in an auto manufacturing plant and we had food, but little else. As kids, we wore second-hand clothes and during hard times, we only had vegetables to eat. I was so ashamed of being so poor."

Norma Jac laughed out loud.

"Oh, honey," she continued in a slight southern drawl, "my life was just the opposite. I was ashamed of being rich."

Karina looked at her.

"I was born with a silver spoon in my mouth," Norma Jac continued. "My daddy owned everything in the little South Georgia town I grew up in. He owned the hardware store, the grocery store, the feed and farm supply company, two insurance companies, and the local auto dealership. Most of my classmates at school were poor as Job's turkey. Every year, my daddy would get a new Chrysler and, when we would get it, I would sit low in the seat because I didn't want my classmates to see me in an expensive new car. I was afraid they would think I felt I was better than them."

Karina burst out laughing.

"That's a great story," she said.

J.L. sat and listened. Outside the window, he could see the cotton fields of south Tennessee rolling past.

"What about your family?" Norma Jac asked.

"My father was Spanish and my mother was Mexican," she said. "My mother was a dancer in Mexican movies when she was young. She grew up in a little coastal town called Zihuatanejo—"

"Oh, I know Zihuatanejo," Norma Jac interjected. "Beautiful little town on the Pacific Coast. There's a basketball court in the town square. Best seafood I ever had."

"My father met my mother during a Cinco de Mayo festival and took her back to Guatemala," Karina said. "I have three sisters."

"Three sisters?" Norma Jac repeated. "That's a lot of girls."

"Well, actually," Karina back-pedaled, "I only have two sisters."

Norma Jac looked at her.

"My youngest sister got pregnant when she was thirteen," Karina said. "After she had the baby, my mother and father told the rest of the world that the child was theirs, so I had a new sister."

Norma Jac laughed.

"Yes, that's a common practice in Europe," Norma Jac said, "Especially in Spain."

"When my uncles saw the baby," Karina continued, "they asked, 'Where did that baby come from?' They would look at me and ask, 'Karina, is that your baby?'"

Norma Jac laughed out loud.

"'Oh, no, it's not my baby!' I would say," Karina continued. "My mother told everybody that she and my father had adopted the child through the church. She said the child was from California and was a relative of Elizabeth Taylor. She named the child Elizabeth."

They rode quietly for several minutes.

"In my family, I was the oldest," Norma Jac said. "Then there was Bill, J.L.'s friend and Della Mae, my youngest sister."

J.L. continued to listen behind them.

"My daddy was always unhappy with Bill," she continued. "Since he was the oldest boy, Daddy always wanted Bill to go to the University of Georgia and be a lawyer, but Bill had no interest. All he ever wanted to do was be around horses and the rodeo. He did try. Bill went up to Athens, enrolled in pre-law, and lasted a month. When he came back home and told Daddy, my father said, 'Son, you'll never amount to anything riding the rodeo. It's a dead-end profession.'

"'That's what I love to do,' he told my daddy. 'I'd rather have my happiness than all the money in the world.'

"My daddy shook his head sadly and never mentioned it again."

They rode quietly.

"When was the last time you talked to Bill?" J.L. asked from the back seat.

"What?" Norma Jac said, turning to look at J.L.

"When was the last time you talked to Bill?" he asked again.

"Didn't you know?" she asked, turning around to look him

in the face.

"Know what?"

She didn't answer at first. "Bill is dead," she said.

"What?" J.L. said. "Bill is dead?"

The woman could hear the shock in his voice.

There was a long pause. "He took his own life three years ago," Norma Jac said finally.

"My God!" J.L. said, more shock in his voice. "What happened?"

"After he got too old to do rodeo, he never could find himself again," Norma Jac said. "He tried lots of different things. Construction, selling cars, doing landscaping—he even worked as a cook for a while. Finally, he just stopped trying and started drinking. It seemed like the only time you would ever see him smile was when he was drinking."

In the back, J.L. was waiting for the shock of the news to register.

They rode quietly.

"How did he do it?" J.L. asked finally.

"Do what?"

"Take his life."

"I would rather not talk about it," Norma Jac said.

J.L. leaned over the back of the seat.

"Please tell me," J.L. pleaded. "He was one of the best friends I ever had. I have to know. Please tell me."

The red-haired woman didn't answer at first. Finally, she cleared her throat. "He put a gun in his mouth," she said, "and pulled the trigger."

"My God," J.L. said sadly. "I would never have dreamed that Bill would do something like that. He loved living too much."

Norma Jac didn't reply.

"In all my life, I've never seen a more persistent person than Bill," J.L. said. "Once when we were at a rodeo in Utah, some cowboys brought in this wild mustang they had captured on the plains. From the moment that horse came to the ranch, nobody could ride it. A cowboy would mount it and come right off. Well, Bill started working with it. The first few days, it would throw Bill right off. Bill would hobble the horse and try again—and try again and try again. Bill outlasted that mustang. I remember after about eight days, the horse saw that Bill wasn't going to give up. On the eighth day, that mustang just quit bucking all together. I mean, he never bucked again. I mean, he never bucked again. That mustang knew he was beaten."

The car was quiet as it rolled southeastward through Alabama toward Atlanta.

"He was always so particular with his hat," J.L. reminisced. "'A cowboy is defined by his hat,' he would say. He once paid $230 for a white Stetson we saw in Dallas. That was a whole week's pay. 'A cowboy looks only as good as his hat,' he said. Sometimes, he would stand in front of the mirror for hours adjusting it this way and that way to get the best effect."

The three rode quietly.

"Once in Kansas," J.L. continued, his voice breaking, "Charley Mason was bulldogging a steer when a bull got loose from the pen and went after Charley. That bull was tossing Charley around like a rag doll. The clowns couldn't get the bull off Charley, so Bill threw a rope around its neck and started winding the rope around its body. After a few seconds, the bull was so tangled up, it just dropped to the ground. We had a big crowd that day and they roared—I mean, they roared—when Bill brought that bull down."

J.L. stopped and started laughing out loud.

"And then there was Cindy," J.L. reminisced. "Every time we would hit Denver, he would go straight to the Lost Corral bar. There was a little brunette there that tended bar. Bill was in love with her. Every year, he would meet her there. Then, one summer we went to Denver and she wasn't there. Oh God, I thought he was going to die. Even then, I would never have dreamed that he would take his own life. He was the best friend I ever had. Rest in peace, my friend."

All the time J.L. had been remembering his friend, the two

women remained silent in the front seat.

"I'm sorry," J.L. said finally. "I guess I'm too emotional sometimes."

"It's okay," Norma Jac said. "I understand how much you cared for my brother," she said. "He spoke of you many, many times. Always with fondness and respect."

They rode quietly.

"Habla español?" Karina asked.

"Sí," Norma Jac replied. "Hablo mucho español."

"Dónde aprendiste?"

"A la Universidad de Georgia y en mi viajando," Norma Jac replied.

"What are y'all talking about up there?" J.L. asked, much calmer now.

"Oh, honey," Norma Jac replied. "It's just girl talk. I'm really enjoying your friend here. Don't pay any attention to us. We'll be in Atlanta in a little while."

***

Two hours later, the late model sedan was on I-20, cruising due east. Ahead of them, they saw a sign: Atlanta city limits. Some eight miles away, they could see the skyscrapers and the rising skyline of downtown Atlanta.

"When we get into downtown Atlanta," Norma Jac said, "I want y'all to go down and meet my sister, Della Mae. She runs the Gone with the Wind museum on Peachtree. She's never met J.L. and she'll probably give you a free tour of the museum."

She looked at Karina.

"You ever read *Gone with the Wind*?" Norma Jac asked.

"Oh yes," Karina said. "I've read it and seen the movie four or five times. You know, I could have been a Southern belle."

"Oh, honey," Norma Jac said with a big laugh, "couldn't we all?"

***

Fifteen minutes later, they were cruising through the twisting, winding concrete canyons of downtown Atlanta.

Finally, Norma Jac turned the late model sedan onto Peachtree Avenue and stopped in front of a white, 19th-century building with a wrap-around porch and a tin roof. Atop the building, a sign proclaimed: Gone with the Wind Museum. On one side was a color photo of Rhett and Scarlett. On the other were face shots of Mammy and Ashley Wilkes.

"I got to run over to the Chamber of Commerce," Norma Jac said. "Y'all go in there and tell Dellie...." She stopped. "No," she said, "let me write a note."

She rummaged through her purse, found a pen, and started scribbling a note. She read the note aloud as she scribbled.

"Dellie:

> J.L. and Karina are friends of mine. J.L. is Bill's best friend from his rodeo days. I know you've heard Bill talk of J.L. at some point. They're traveling to Florida and need a room for the night. Please provide accommodations to them.

Norma Jac"

With that, she signed the note and handed it to Karina. "Go in there and give this to Dellie Mae," she said.

"Thank you so much," Karina said. "I'm so happy to meet you. I feel like I've known you all my life."

"Oh, honey, and I feel the same way," Norma Jac said.

Karina leaned over in the seat and hugged Norma Jac.

"Y'all take care," Norma Jac said as they got out of the car.

"Thanks for the ride," J.L. said.

"Y'all are welcome," the woman said.

J.L. and Karina watched as the car sped off down Peachtree Avenue.

Nighttime at the Museum

Moments later, J.L. and Karina were walking up the steps of the museum building. At the door, Karina stopped and knocked. No answer. For a moment, they looked around the premises to see if anyone was around.

Karina knocked again.

Inside, they could hear someone unlocking the door. The door opened and a woman stuck her head out.

"The museum is closed," she said.

"Do you know Dellie Mae Shoulders?" Karina asked.

The woman peered at them curiously.

"I'm Dellie Mae," she said.

She stepped out on the porch and closed the door behind her.

"A red-headed lady named Norma Jac Shoulders brought us from Memphis to Atlanta," Karina said. "She said you could give us a room for the night."

The woman stared incredulously at Karina.

"What?" she said, her face screwing up in disbelief.

"She sent this note," Karina said. "She said you were her sister."

Karina handed her the note. The woman took the note and looked at them skeptically. Then, as she read the note, a terrified look flashed across her face. "And it's her signature!" the woman screamed again, dropping, almost throwing the note on the porch floor in horror.

"What's wrong?" J.L. said, picking up the note.

"We're sorry," Karina said. "We didn't mean to frighten you."

"Who are you people?" the woman asked frantically.

J.L. explained again that he was her brother Bill's rodeo friend and her sister had brought them from Memphis to Atlanta.

The woman peered at them.

"My sister Norma Jac has been dead six years," the woman explained. "She was killed in an auto accident just outside of Memphis in 2001."

Karina looked at J.L. He didn't say anything. "So who was the red-haired woman we were talking to for the last three hours?" Karina asked.

Dellie Mae didn't answer. She looked at them. Then, she took the note back from J.L. She read it again and again.

"Y'all come on," she said finally. "There is no way I can ignore something like this."

She started inside the museum building with J.L. and Karina. Then, she stopped and looked at the note again.

"That's her signature, all right," the woman said with disbelief. "And the ink is fresh."

She looked up from the note again and peered curiously at them.

"Are you people some kind of angels?" she asked.

Karina shrugged.

"Come on," Dellie Mae said again. "I've got to help you people."

***

Ten minutes later, she was leading J.L. and Karina, suitcases in hand, to the rear of the museum.

"There are some old servant's quarters back here," she said. "They haven't been used in years, but it's clean and dry and you're welcome to stay the night."

She stopped in front of a room and unlocked the door. Inside, Karina saw a neatly made bed, a writing table, a sitting area, and a bathroom.

"This is great!" Karina said. "Thanks so much."

"Is this your husband?" Della Mae asked.

Karina shook her head.

"Then I'll give him the room next door," she said.

119

She produced a key and opened the door to the adjacent room.

"Here's the key," she said, handing it to J.L. "It's just like this one."

"Thanks," J.L. said.

The woman stared at them and then turned to go. After taking several steps, she stopped and turned again. She still wasn't satisfied.

"What did Norma Jac look like?" she asked.

"Oh, she had a mountain of red hair," Karina said. "She was well-dressed and was smiling and laughing the whole time we talked. She told me about studying Spanish in Mexico and Central America and about her childhood in South Georgia. Probably the nicest person I ever met.

Again, Dellie Mae peered at them incredulously.

Okay," she said finally. "Have a good night. You can buy food in the machines. Remember to drop the key in the back door slot when you leave tomorrow."

For a moment, the women peered curiously again at them, then visibly shivered. Finally, she turned and started walking back to the front of the museum.

***

Inside his room, J.L. was unpacked and preparing for bed. Suddenly, there was a knock on the door.

"Who is it?" he asked.

"It's me," Karina answered.

He opened the door.

Karina, dressed in her nightclothes, flew into his arms the moment he opened the door. She was trembling with fright. He held her for a moment.

"Cowboy! Cowboy!" she said frantically. "This place is haunted. Let's get out of here."

"Where would we go?" J.L. asked. "We have a room here for the night."

"I'm afraid to stay here," she said. "This is too spooky. We talked to that woman for three hours, then.... Can I sleep in here tonight?"

120

He could see she was trembling with fear.

"I guess so," he said.

"Will you go back to my room to get my suitcase?"

"Are you that scared?"

"Oh, God, yes!" she said.

"Okay, stay here," he said. "I'll be right back."

Moments later, he returned with her suitcase.

"Oh, I'm so afraid," she said. "Will you hold me?"

J.L. peered into her eyes, then for no reason, she began passionately kissing him. Without hesitation, her kisses were turned in kind.

"Oh, cowboy," she said. "I've waited a long time for this."

She was breathing hard. She could feel his erection between them. She started to unbutton his shirt as he passionately kissed her neck. Now he was breathing hard and his hand moved to her breast. Suddenly, he stopped.

"What's wrong?" she asked.

"We shouldn't be doing this..."

"Don't you like me?"

"Yes, I like you," he replied. "I like you a lot and I think I would enjoy you, but I'm afraid to do this."

"Afraid of what?

"I'm just not sure that I'm ready to turn myself loose with a woman again," he said. "I've only known you for six days."

She stopped.

"We shouldn't go rushing into anything," he continued.

From the look on her face, you could she was in agreement with what he said.

"Maybe you're right," she said.

He pulled away from her and started re-buttoning his shirt.

"Maybe later, but not right now," he said. "I've only known you a few days. There is not enough karma between us."

She looked away dejectedly.

"Then just hold me," she said. "I need your strength tonight."

Again, he took her into his arms and held her for a long

moment. He liked the feel of her. She felt so warm and comfortable in his arms. Suddenly, he could feel his passion yearning to be released. He had to contain his emotions. This was not the time to be jumping off any cliffs.

J.L. broke the embrace.

"Okay," he said, "We'll sleep together tonight, but we can't do anything too hot and heavy. When the time is right, if the time becomes right, we'll do it. Not until then."

Again, he could see the dejection in her eyes.

"You're a very strange person," she said. "Unlike any man I've ever known."

He shook his head and looked away.

"Come on," he said. "Let's get some sleep..."

***

When he awoke the next morning, her body, still dressed in a flimsy nightgown, was nestled close to his. Her arms were wrapped tightly around his waist, her hands clasped over his belly button. It had been two years since a woman's body had been that close to his. He liked the feeling of warmth, but he was afraid of where it might lead. Carefully, he unclasped her hands from around his waist and got out of bed. She awoke.

"Is it morning?" she asked.

"Yeah," he said. "We need to get up and get started."

***

Thirty minutes later, their suitcases were repacked and, as instructed, they left their room keys in the back door slot. Once outside on the street, they scanned the area. Ahead of them, at the corner, J.L. saw a sign with an arrow. It read: Outman City Park.

"Come on," he said. "Let's walk down to the park."

For some fifteen minutes, suitcases in hand, they walked silently.

"Why are you so quiet?" she asked finally.

"I can't believe Bill is dead," he said. "One of the best friends I ever had in all my life. I would never have dreamed that he would kill himself. I'm going to have to start paying more attention to my spirituality."

"Your what?"

"My sense of spirituality," he said. "My sense of death and the afterlife."

She looked at him, then continued walking.

DeWayne II

Ahead of them, they could see a public park. Along the sidewalk, they saw an assortment of artists displaying their wares, street entertainers, and displays of jewelry, trinkets, and custom clothing. J.L. stopped and examined some of the paintings. Karina stopped with him.

"Hey, cowboy," he heard someone call.

J.L. turned and looked in the direction of the voice. Some twenty feet away, between a street singer and a juggling act, he saw DeWayne, the fat preacher he had met at Little Big Horn. Nearby, resting on a recliner, was the old Indian man. J.L. walked over.

J.L. shook hands with him. DeWayne saw Karina.

"Did you get married since the last time I saw you?" he asked facetiously.

"Oh no," J.L. replied. "She's just a friend. This is Karina."

DeWayne greeted her.

"The show is about to go on," DeWayne said. "Can you help me with him?"

Moments later, J.L. and DeWayne had the old Indian, hat in hand, seated on the fake tree stump in front of a gathering crowd.

The marquee had a different pitch than before. This time, he billed the old Indian as "Chief Lone Pine of the great Cherokee tribe." The same photos were displayed as before.

Once the old Indian was seated, a crowd, including several families with small children, had gathered to stare at him. The crowd grew quiet and the old Indian raised his hand.

"Since many, many moons, my people lived peacefully on these lands," he said. "Then the white man came and killed our people and took what remained of us on great Trail of Tears to reservation in Oklahoma. On reservation, we have no wildlife, no land to grow food, and we have to eat rat."

The old Indian looked at a well-dressed woman in the crowd.

"You ever eat rat?" the old Indian asked.

"Oh no!" the woman said in horror.

Suddenly, the old Indian's hand fell; he grabbed his chest, dropped the hat, and fell off the stump. The crowd withdrew in horror.

Dewayne rushed over.

"Give him some air! Give him some air," he said. "He's old and frail."

DeWayne fanned the old Indian with a Bible and held the hat for donations.

"Oh, that poor Indian," said one man, and he dropped some bills in the hat.

"I hope this helps," a young woman said, dropping more bills in the hat.

"May God bless that poor Indian," said an older black woman, opening her purse and dropping some bills in the hat.

After several more people dropped money in the hat, the crowd dispersed.

DeWayne bent over the prostrate Indian.

"Chief," he said, "get up! The crowd is gone now."

The old Indian didn't move.

"Chief, get up," DeWayne said again, shaking the old Indian's shoulders.

There was no response.

"Chief! Chief!" DeWayne said again. "Can you hear me?"

DeWayne put his hand under the old Indian's nostril.

He wasn't breathing.

"Damn!" DeWayne said. "He's gone this time. I mean, he's really gone to the Happy Hunting Ground."

"He's dead?" J.L. asked.

"Yep, looks that way," DeWayne said. "He ain't breathing. Well, so much for the casino in Cabazon."

"What are you going to do?" J.L. asked.

"I'll have to call the coroner to come and get him," DeWayne said sadly. "It's really a shame. Me and him made a lot of easy money together."

For a moment, he stared sadly at the old Indian and then he turned back to J.L. and Karina.

"Where y'all headed?" he asked.

"We're going to Florida," J.L. replied.

"Where's your truck?" DeWayne asked.

"It was stolen," J.L. replied.

"So you ain't got wheels?"

J.L. nodded.

"I'm headed down to Valdosta to sell some Bibles. Y'all want to ride with me in the van?"

"Sure," J.L. said. "If it's okay."

"No problem!" Dewayne said. "I've got to talk to the coroner's office and then we'll go."

***

Thirty minutes later, as Karina, J.L., and the crowd watched, a coroner's office rep arrived, covered the old Indian's body with a sheet, and transported it into a waiting van. He slammed the door to the van and produced an official-looking document.

"Are you Chief Lone Pine's only living relative?" he asked.

"Looks that way," DeWayne said.

"Sign here," he said, handing DeWayne the document and a pen.

DeWayne took the document and pen.

"What y'all going to do with him?" DeWayne asked. "Put him in a potter's field?"

"Oh no!" the coroner's rep said. "We have to follow the federal law to the letter on Indians. The Native American Heritage act of 1976 requires that he be buried with all the same ceremony he would receive if he were still with his native tribe. Since he was Cherokee, he will lie in state for three days and have the smoky buzzard ceremony performed twice every three hours. Then, there will be the eagle's blessing with all of the native drums and death dance ceremony to prepare his soul for transport to the next world. Finally, there will be the water cleaning ceremony, which will last another day, and then we'll transport him to the official Cherokee burial ground in North Carolina."

"Isn't all that kind of expensive?" DeWayne asked.

"About $27,000," the coroner's assistant said. "It's a federal law. We have to do it. Taxpayers pick up the tab."

DeWayne shrugged.

He signed the paper, handed it back to the coroner's rep, and turned to J.L. and Karina.

"Y'all ready?"

***

Two hours later, J.L. and Karina were cruising south down I-75 in DeWayne's old blue van. J.L. was in the passenger seat and Karina was in the back seat among the Bibles and Indian paraphernalia.

"When I was growing up in South Georgia," DeWayne said, "I could see that my life was already cut out for me. Early on, my parents expected me to follow in my daddy's footsteps and farm the 8,000 acres of cotton that my father's family had been doing for five generations. I never said anything, but I knew I wasn't going to spend my life farming cotton. It was the same thing year after year. There would be cutting plows and fertilizer and planters in March and April. In June and July, there would be tillers and cultivators. Then, in August and September, there would be the cotton pickers. I used to see my daddy come in from the field after twelve hours on a cotton picker and he would look like he was near death. He died at fifty-three. I told myself I wasn't going to let that happen to me."

Outside the van window, J.L. could see the highway shops, the manufacturer outlets, the advertisements for free peaches and pecans, and the endless pine forests of central Georgia rolling past.

"Then one day in church," DeWayne continued, "I had a

revelation. I realized that people would pay money—real money—if you told them they didn't have to die and would go to Heaven. Sunday after Sunday, I would watch as they passed the plate. People would put in tens and twenties and sometimes you'd even see a fifty go in. I knew I was going to have some of that. So I sent off in the mail and got ordained as a preacher by this outfit up in Tennessee. Rev. DeWayne William Carter, the paper said. That meant I could legally have my own church."

"How long you been with the chief?" J.L. asked.

"About three years," DeWayne said. "I met him in Oklahoma when I was traveling with the Methodists."

"I thought you were Baptist?" J.L. said.

"Well, that's what I call myself," DeWayne said, "but it's all the same."

They rode quietly.

"Are you and her..." DeWayne didn't finish the sentence.

"Are we what?" J.L. replied.

"You know..." DeWayne said, "...romantically involved?"

"No!" J.L. said. "We're just friends. Traveling companions."

DeWayne looked at Karina in the rearview mirror.

"What kind of work do you do?" he asked her.

"I'm a Spanish teacher," she said.

"Cómo está?" he said.

She didn't answer.

"You don't like to speak Spanish?" Dewayne asked. "I thought that was all they spoke in Mexico."

"I'm not from Mexico," she said curtly.

"You look like a Mexican," he said.

Karina didn't reply.

"You got a sister in Mexico?" he asked, winking at J.L.

"I told you," Karina said, "I'm not from Mexico."

They rode quietly.

The van was now deep in South Georgia. On either side of I-75, J.L. could see signs for souvenir shops, boiled peanuts, canned peaches, and pecan candies rolling past.

"You think you could teach me Spanish?" DeWayne asked.

"Probably not," she said curtly.

"Would you be interested in a business deal?" he asked.

"What do you have in mind?" she replied.

He looked back at her.

"Now that the chief is gone," he said, "I'm looking for a new gig. You know, me and you could go down to Miami and make some big money on the streets. Those white men at South Beach, they love Mexican women." He reached his hand over the back seat and patted her knee.

"Get your hands off me!" she shouted angrily.

After seeing what DeWayne had done, J.L. turned angrily to him in the front seat and grabbed a fistful of his shirt.

"Stop the car! Stop the car, you goddamn redneck!" J.L. shouted. "Stop the frickin' car!"

"Cowboy! Cowboy!" DeWayne said apologetically. "I didn't mean to piss you off. You said there was nothing between the two of you."

"Stop the Goddamn car," J.L. shouted angrily, holding DeWayne's shirt and shaking him violently, "or I'll beat the holy crap out of you."

"Okay, okay," DeWayne said. "I'm stopping. I'm stopping."

The car screeched to a halt.

J.L. released his shirt and started to get out.

"You fricking redneck!" J.L. shouted, glaring angrily. "You're lucky I don't beat the hell out of you. You understand me?"

"Yes, sir! Yes, sir!" DeWayne replied.

With that, J.L. and Karina got out of the van and slammed the door.

Once outside the van, J.L. and Karina waited for him to move on. "Go on," J.L. said, motioning him to get back on the road.

"Hey, cowboy," DeWayne called.

J.L. looked at him.

"This is for you," he said, showing him a middle finger.

"Just go on," J.L. said. "Just go on about your own business."

With that, the blue van sped off down the highway.

Selma

Ten minutes later, J.L. and Karina, suitcases in hand, were walking down a long stretch of a desolate, two-lane, South Georgia highway. In either direction, all they could see was asphalt, the South Georgia sky, and pine trees. No houses. No cars. Nobody.

"Thanks for trying to protect me back there," Karina said as they walked.

"I was sick and tired of his redneck crap," J.L. replied.

To the east, J.L. could see giant thunderheads building.

"It's going to be pouring here in a few minutes," he said.

"Yeah, looks that way," she said.

As they walked, it began to mist and then drizzle. After about ten minutes of drizzling, it started to downpour.

"Let's see if we can find some shelter," he said.

They walked for another twenty minutes. Both were soaking wet.

Karina sat down on the wet ground.

"Oh, cowboy, I'm so tired," she said. "I didn't sleep well last night. I feel awful."

He noticed she was shivering.

"You're getting sick," he said. "Come on; we've got to keep walking. We'll find some shelter up here somewhere."

J.L. reached down his hand and pulled her to her feet. She started walking again. Ahead of them, he could see a dirt road intersecting the main highway. At the intersection, he saw a bank of mailboxes and a school bus stop with a shelter.

"Let's see if we can get to the school bus shelter up there," he said, pointing in the distance.

She didn't hear anything he said. She took two more steps and then collapsed on the ground again.

"I can't go any further," she said. "I am so sick. Every part of me hurts."

"Come on," J.L. said. "Let's see if we can make it to that school bus stop."

J.L. could see she was helpless. Quickly, he picked her up, threw her over his shoulder, and carried her and both suitcases the final fifty yards to the bus stop. She was unconscious. The rain was whipping about, but the inside of the bus stop was dry. For several minutes, he sat on the bench and held her head in his lap and watched the swirling rain. He saw a pickup truck appear on the dirt road across from the bus stop.

The pickup pulled out on the highway and then stopped at the bank of mailboxes to collect mail from one of the boxes. The rain was so hard and so heavy that J.L. couldn't see the driver. For a moment, the pickup remained in front of the mailboxes and then started backing up. J.L watched as the pickup stopped in front of the bus stop.

A tall black woman wearing glasses, with salt and pepper hair, and in her late seventies got out. She slammed the pickup door, opened an umbrella, and rushed through the rain to the bus stop.

"My Lord!" she said, rain dripping off of her umbrella. "What happened to her?"

"She's sick," J.L. said. "Really sick."

The old woman bent over her, looked at her Karina's pupils, and then put her hand on her forehead to feel her temperature.

"Yeah, she's sick all right," the old black woman concluded. "Are you her husband?"

"No, I'm just a friend."

The woman looked back at Karina.

"She's going to have to have some help or she's going to get pneumonia and die," the woman said.

J.L. looked at her, saying nothing.

"Come on!" she said. "Let me see if I can't help y'all. Can you help me get her in the truck?"

J.L. picked up Karina again and carried her through the

driving rain to the pickup while the old woman held the door. Then, he put her into the truck seat, got in, and slammed the door behind him.

Moments later, J.L. and the old black woman were in the pickup, bouncing aimlessly over a pothole-filled dirt road. Karina was slumped unconscious against J.L. in the front seat.

"You're lucky I found you," the woman said. "She's really sick. My name is Selma," she said. "You and she can stay at my house tonight. I'm a midwife and a nurse. I'll have her up and going again in a couple days. Where are y'all going?"

"To Florida," J.L. said.

"Do you know how to milk a goat?"

"I know how to milk a cow," J.L. replied.

"Same difference," she said. "Can you help me out some in return?"

"That's the least I can do," J.L. said.

"Are you a real cowboy?" she asked.

"I'm a real cowboy," he replied.

***

Finally, the old pickup pulled into the front yard of a small farmhouse tucked away in a grove of tall Georgia pines. Beside the house, J.L. could see a large garden plot and a chicken house. Directly behind the house, there was a barn with a hayloft and some twenty goats inside a sheltered pen. Once the truck stopped, J.L. carried Karina into the house while the old black woman carried their suitcases. Once inside, she directed J.L. into a front bedroom. J.L. gently laid Karina on the bed.

"Leave us alone," the old woman said. "I was a nurse for eighteen years, so I'll handle this from here."

"Thank you," J.L. said. "Got a place where I can put on some dry clothes?"

"Go into the second bedroom," she said, indicating to the right. "You can change in there."

***

An hour later, Karina was sleeping soundly in the front bedroom. Selma had removed her wet clothes and put her in

133

an old flowery nightgown and fed her warm goat's milk, some chicken broth, and some crackers.

"This child is really sick," Selma said. "She's probably going to need a doctor."

"We've got eighteen dollars to our name," J.L. said. "Unless the doctor will accept a credit card."

Selma looked at him.

"Let me see if I don't have some antibiotics left over from the bout with the flu I had last winter."

She got up and went to the kitchen. Moments later, she returned with a bottle of pills.

"We're in luck," she said. "Leave me with her."

With that, J.L. turned and went into the front room.

"Honey, wake up," she said, shaking Karina's shoulder.

Karina opened her eyes and looked around.

"Where am I?" she asked, genuinely frightened. "What is all of this?"

"Now just stay calm," Selma said. "You're really sick. I want you to take these pills."

"Where's Cowboy?" Karina asked.

"He's in the front room," she said. "J.L., come in here," Selma called. "Your friend wants you."

J.L. appeared from the other room.

Karina reached her arms out to him and he sat on the bed and took her in his arms.

Selma watched. "Are you sure you two aren't more than good friends?"

"Where am I?" Karina said drowsily, looking into J.L.'s face.

"This is Selma," J.L. said. "We're at her house. She brought us here from the school bus stop. She's going to try to get you well."

Karina looked at Selma.

"Thank you so much," Karina said drowsily.

"I've got five antibiotic tablets here," Selma said. "Are you allergic to anything?"

"Not that I know of," Karina replied.

"I want you to take two now, one again in five hours, and then another in another five hours. You're sick, child. I mean, really sick."

"Yes, I know," Karina said. "I feel terrible."

She took the two pills Selma offered her and put them in her mouth.

"Now have some of this warm goat's milk," Selma said.

As instructed, Karina gulped down a swig of goat's milk after the pills.

"Now you need to rest," Selma said. "If you get hungry, just holler. I've got plenty of chicken noodle soup on the stove. Me and J.L. will be here to watch after you."

"Thank you so much," Karina said.

Moments later, Karina was sound asleep again.

***

J.L. and Selma went to the barn to milk the goats. She said she had nine goats that were producing milk. She explained that several others were producing, but there wasn't enough milk there to mess with. As J.L. milked the goats, he noticed that the goat's front udders were larger than a cow's, but the back udders were smaller than a cow's. *There must be some sort of genetic explanation for that*, he thought. Later, while Selma finished milking the last goat, J.L. threw several bales of hay from the barn loft into the goats' stalls.

An hour after they started, Selma and J.L. together had milked four gallons of fresh goat's milk. Once they had finished the milking, Selma took the fresh milk inside and strained it one gallon at a time through straining cloths.

"Goat's milk is a lot better for you than cow's milk," Selma said. "It has more fat than cow's milk, but it also has lots of natural antibiotics in it. You know, with this goat's milk and those left-over antibiotics, I'll have your friend up and going again by tomorrow."

After the goat's milk was stored away, Selma started preparing fried chicken, mashed potatoes, and lima beans, with cornbread and iced tea. Finally, after J.L. had set the table, the meal was ready and they prepared to eat. Selma blessed the food and they started eating.

"You know, you're the first white man that's been in this house in over twenty years," she said. "I have a niece named Shakira that lives up north. She visited me long ago and brought her white husband with her. I never had a reason to not like white folks," she said. "Most of them I ever knew were just like black folks, if you know what I mean."

J.L. nodded as he took a bite of fried chicken.

"How long you been in this house?" he asked.

"Longer than you're old," Selma said. "Been here since 1958. When I was sixteen, that would have been 1956, my daddy took me over to his sister Willa Mae's house and introduced me to Clarence. Before we got there, my daddy said Clarence was the man he wanted me to marry. Well, we never did really get married, but we told everybody we did. When we decided to join up together, I told him I wanted a house and a place to have a garden, some chickens, and some young 'uns. At the time, Clarence worked for Mr. Wade Hollis over in Valdosta and he owned over 10,000 acres in these parts. Mr. Wade told Clarence that if he would tend his cattle for a year, he would give him this house and five acres. Clarence took him up on it. So we moved in here in the spring of '58. Clarence did pretty good fulfilling my requests, I'll say that for him. He was a good worker and he knew how to manage money, but some paydays, and I never knew why, he would go off and get drunk and gamble it away. I never did understand that. He died in '92."

J.L. nodded. He was wolfing down a piece of strawberry cobbler.

"We raised four kids," Selma continued. "They're all gone now. I got certified to be a nurse over in Albany after the kids were gone. Spent eleven years nursing old folks in Valdosta. I turned out to be a pretty good nurse, if I say so myself."

"You seem to really know what you're doing with Karina," J.L. said. "I thank you so much."

"I always loved to help people," Selma said. "I always feel better about myself when I help others."

The two fell silent for a moment.

J.L. noticed a photo on the mantel of a very young Selma posing with a group of African-Americans.

"What is this photo?" he asked.

"Oh, that's my photo with Dr. King," she said. "In 1963, I was twenty-three years old and me and Clarence and other members of our church went up to Atlanta to march for civil rights. Dr. King said he had a dream that black folks should have all the same rights that white people had.

"Well, after the marching was finished and President Johnson passed all of his bills in Washington, things did get better. A lot better. Black folks started getting good jobs and driving new cars and owning nice homes. Black folks started appearing in television and in magazines and things definitely got better for them. Now they've even elected a black president. But I'll tell you, I've never seen kids like these kids today. Never ever. All these kids know nowadays is drugs and violence and shooting and time in prison. Some things got better, but some things got worse. Much, much worse."

Selma got up from the table.

"I'm going to wash these dishes and I'm going to bed," she said. "You better stay in your friend's room tonight in case she wakes up and needs something."

Throughout the night, J.L stayed at Karina's bedside, dozing intermittently in a recliner. He had strict instructions from Selma to give her more goat's milk and another antibiotic tablet if she woke up.

Around midnight, Karina woke up.

"How you feeling?" J.L. asked.

"A lot better," she said. "Where's the black lady?"

"She's asleep," he said. "Take this pill and wash it down with this goat's milk."

She did as instructed and, moments later, she was fast asleep again.

***

The following morning, J.L. and Selma were up at daybreak. After about an hour, they had milked and fed the goats again.

"Will you do me a big favor?" she asked.

"Sure," J.L. said. "Anything you ask."

"Will you clean out that front stall and throw some new hay in there?"

"Got a shovel?" J.L. asked.

"It's in the tool shed," Selma said.

For over an hour, J.L. worked shoveling the dirt and manure out of the stall. It had been a long time since he had a shovel in his hand. Reminded him of his childhood days in Oklahoma. Finally, the stall was clean and he took half a bale of hay from the barn and strewed it about the now clean stall.

***

Back inside, J.L. found Selma at the kitchen table, straining goat's milk.

"I'm going to make some predictions."

"What's that?" J.L. asked.

"I predict that your lady friend is going to come out of that room any minute now and go to the bathroom. After using the bathroom, she's going to need about fifteen minutes to come out here fully dressed and suitcase in hand just rarin' to go."

J.L. laughed.

"We'll see," he said.

Sure enough, eight minutes later, Karina came out of the bedroom, went to the bathroom, and then returned to the bedroom.

Fourteen minutes later, she appeared in the kitchen, fully dressed and suitcase in hand.

J.L. smiled at Selma.

"I been a nurse a long, long time," she said confidently, looking at J.L. "Those leftover antibiotics did the trick."

"You definitely know what you're doing," J.L. said.

The three of them had a breakfast of sausage and eggs and hot biscuits.

"You're an angel from heaven," Karina said as they ate.

"Like I told your friend here, I know good people when I see 'em," Selma said. "Besides, it gets lonely around here sometimes. Sometimes I like some company."

They continued to eat.

"Before y'all leave, I want you to take a ride with me over in the woods."

"What?" Karina asked.

"You know, my grandson flies the U.S. mail back and forth between here and Florida," she said. "Now I'm not sure how close he goes to where y'all are going, but we can ask."

J.L. looked at Karina.

"It's worth a try," she said.

Drug Dealers

An hour later, Selma's pickup, with J.L and Karina and their suitcases in tow, was winding along an uneven dirt road through the piney back woods of South Georgia. Finally, the truck stopped in a heavily wooded area that had a small landing strip. Selma parked the truck and she, J.L., and Karina got out. Ahead of them, they saw a small, four-seater airplane. A young black man had his head stuck inside the plane's raised engine hood. When he heard the truck door slam, he withdrew his head and started walking toward them while wiping his hands on a cloth.

"Grandma, what are you doing here?" he asked.

"Darryl, I want you to meet J.L. and Karina," she said.

"Hi," Darryl said, giving J.L. and Karina a weak greeting. "Grandma, I told you to never bring people around here."

"This is a special case," Selma said.

He was obviously irritated.

"Okay, Grandma," he said resignedly. "What is it?"

"These people are going to Florida," she said. "They've come all the way across the USA and they got a little further to go."

"What do you want me to do?" Darryl asked.

"I want you to let them ride with you to Florida," she said. Turning to J.L., she asked, "Where did you say you were going?"

"Port Everglades," J.L. said.

"That's close to where I'm going," Darryl said, "but I can't take any passengers. It's against the rules. You know, FAA and all that."

"Look!" the grandmother said, irritation growing in her voice.

"No, Grandma," Darryl said, cutting her short. "I can't do it. I could get in lots of trouble."

"It won't hurt you or anybody else to let these people ride in the back of your plane while you deliver the mail," she said. "It'll help these people and you'll be creating some good karma."

"No! No! No! No!" Darryl said. "A thousand times—no!"

Selma decided to try another tack.

"I'll make you another sweet potato pie," she said sweetly.

"Sweet potato pie?" Darryl said, his eyes lighting up with interest.

"Yep," the grandmother replied.

He studied his grandmother for an instant.

"Do you like sweet potato pie?" Karina asked.

"Oh, I love it!" Darryl said.

"I just happen to have a piece," she said. "It kind of old, but it should still be good."

"Oh, I like it old," Darryl said.

Karina opened her suitcase and produced the slab of pie the old religious woman had given them in Memphis.

"My, my; look at that!" he said, eyeing the pie hungrily.

Karina handed it to him.

"What did you say their names was, Grandma?"

"J.L. and Karina," Selma replied.

"How much y'all weigh?" Darryl asked.

"Why do you need that?" Selma asked.

"FAA regulations," Darryl said. "I don't want to overload my plane."

He turned back to J.L. and Karina.

"I'm 185," J.L. said.

"I'm 101 pounds," Karina replied.

Darryl looked at her, smiled, and rolled his eyes.

"Okay," he said. "I think it will be okay. I'm not going all the way to Port Everglades," he said. "I'm going to Palatka, which is about twenty miles north. It'll get you real close to where you're going. Do you want to put your bags in cargo?"

"No, we'll hang on to them," J.L. said.

"Okay, let's go," Darryl said.

"Thank you, honey," the grandmother said delightedly. "Now you take care of these people. These are my friends and they're good people."

"I will, Grandma," he said.

"Goodbye." Selma waved to J.L. and Karina.

"Goodbye," Karina said. "You've been an angel."

With that, J.L. and Karina got inside the small plane.

***

The plane was a four-seater—two seats up front in the cockpit and two seats behind for passengers. J.L. and Karina were seated in the two back seats behind the pilot. There were windows all around and several large canvas bags in the cargo area beside J.L. and Karina. The bags read: U.S. Mail. Property of U.S. Postal Service.

"Y'all buckled in?" Darryl asked.

"Yep," J.L. said.

"Okay," the pilot said. "Here we go!"

Darryl pushed a button and the prop started to spin. The engine roared to life with a loud whirring sound and the plane started to slowly move forward. Moments later, the plane was at the starting point of the landing strip. The low RPM spinning erupted into a much louder roaring sound and the small plane began to gain speed as it raced down the runway. Moments later, the ailerons went up and the plane was aloft.

Inside the plane, Darryl turned to J.L. "Flying one of these things is a piece of cake with computers," Darryl said. "You just push a couple of buttons and the plane flies itself."

"Personally, I haven't had much luck with computers lately," J.L. said.

"Y'all just enjoy the ride," Darryl said. "It's about forty minutes down there."

J.L. relaxed in his seat. Outside the plane window, J.L. could see the endless pine forests and fallow fields of South Georgia below him. He dozed off and then some twenty minutes later, he woke up and glanced below him again. The pine forests and farms had faded away and now the terrain had become an endless collection of palm trees, palmetto fields, and cypress groves with thousands upon thousands of little lakes interspersed. J.L. knew they were in Florida. He could feel the plane getting ready to land as it drifted closer and closer to earth. In front of him in the cockpit, he watched as Darryl punched some keys on a computer keyboard.

Darryl stopped and looked at the computer.

The pilot punched in more numbers.

"Damn! What's wrong with this fricking thing?" Darryl said.

He pulled a paper from the plane's glove compartment and unfolded it.

"Okay," he said, "one more time."

While reading numbers directly off the paper, he punched them into the computer again. Obviously, he wasn't getting the response he expected.

"This damn computer," he said, slamming his fist repeatedly against the keyboard.

Suddenly, the plane veered left. Darryl grabbed the controls and jerked it to the right. Huge sparks and smoke arose from behind the dashboard and the plane went into a steep dive. J.L. and Karina could see flames lapping out of the left side of the plane.

"Oh God! Oh God!!" Karina screamed as the plane started pitching and diving erratically and appeared to be headed straight down into the ground. "We're going to die. We're going to die!"

She grabbed his arm, laid her head on it, and squeezed him with all of her might.

"Hang on!" J.L. said, clinging to the hand strap. "We're not dead yet."

"Oh, cowboy!" she shouted, holding tightly to his arm, her face a mask of fear and horror. "I have to tell you something before I die."

"Can't it wait?" J.L. said, clinging to the hand strap.

"No!" she said. "I've fallen in love with you during all this. You're the kindest, most decent man I've ever known in all my life. I love you."

He looked at her. The plane had leveled off some now, but was wobbling uncontrollably as it moved closer and closer to the earth's surface. In front of them, Darryl was wrestling with the controls, doing everything he could to bring the craft under control. Meanwhile, the flames on the left side of the plane were growing larger.

"Y'all hang on," Darryl shouted. "It's going to be a rough landing."

Ahead of them on the ground, J.L. could see a cow pasture with several Holstein cows grazing peacefully. As the plane started down, the cows looked up from their grazing and then quickly moved out of the plane's path. J.L. could see the earth coming at them very fast.

The plane's wheels hit the ground and the craft bounced several feet in the air. Moments later, it hit the ground again and started rolling erratically across the uneven pasture until it came to rest in a wild blackberry patch. Inside, the plane was filling up with smoke.

In the cockpit, Darryl was still taking his wrath out on the computer.

"This goddamn computer," he said angrily, slamming his fist on the keyboard again and again.

"Come on," J.L. said frantically. "Let's get out of here."

Once he was free of his seatbelt, he helped Karina out of her seat and, suitcases in hand, they bolted out of the plane. Moments later, Darryl, J.L., and Karina were sitting on the ground outside the plane, gasping for breath.

A tall Latin man with slicked-back black hair, a pencil mustache, and wearing a custom-tailored suit, rushed up. He was waving an automatic pistol. Four other Latin men, apparently his minions, rushed up behind them, also waving pistols.

The tall Latin man looked at Darryl.

"What took you so long?" he asked.

"That goddamn computer," Darryl said.

Then the tall Latin man saw J.L. and Karina and turned

back to Darryl.

"Who are these people?" the Latin man asked angrily.

"They're friends of my grandmother," Darryl said.

"Friends of your grandmother?" the tall Latin man asked sarcastically. "They're witnesses. They could get me deported back to Cuba."

One of his minions yelled to him. "Boss! Boss!' he shouted, pointing to the burning plane.

"Ay, Caramba!" he said angrily. He barked quick orders to his men and two of them rushed to the plane. One opened an outside compartment on the plane and pulled out a fire extinguisher. Expertly, the second minion pulled the pin and the extinguisher gave a loud "swoosh" as he applied it to the fire. Moments later, the fire was extinguished.

He turned back to J.L. and Karina.

"Now back to you," he said.

"Boss! Boss!" Another minion pointed. There was smoke billowing out of the plane's cargo area.

"Get the stash!" the boss shouted. "Now!"

With that, the minion with the fire extinguisher rushed back to the plane and sprayed down the new fire. The others started pulling the canvas bags out of the plane. They removed nine canvas bags from the cargo area. Flames had reached one of the bags and its contents had caught fire. J.L. smelled marijuana smoke.

Upon seeing the smoldering canvas bag and the smoking marijuana inside, the Latin man pulled off his tailor-made jacket and beat it against the burning canvas bag until the flames were out.

Then he turned back to J.L. and Karina. As he eyed them, he threw a cartridge into the chamber of his automatic pistol.

He stopped and sniffed. He smelled something and looked down at his shoes.

"Yaaaiiiiiii!" he shouted in anger. "Cow poop on my alligator shoes!"

Instantly, one of his minions was by his side. The tall Latin man removed the shoe and handed it to his minion. The minion took the shoe and, using a handkerchief, wiped the manure off. Then, he handed it back to his boss. The tall Latin man took the shoe cautiously and smelled it. Apparently approving his minion's cleaning job, he put the shoe back on his foot. Then, he turned to J.L. and Karina again.

"Get down on your knees and say your prayers," he ordered.

"Oh, don't shoot us!" Karina pleaded fearfully. "Please don't shoot us!"

Darryl jumped up off the ground and went straight to the tall Latin man.

"Al! Al!" Darryl called. "You can't hurt these people. They're friends of my grandma."

Angrily, Al turned to Darryl. He grabbed a fistful of Darryl's shirt, pulled his face close, and held the cocked automatic to his head.

"You crazy little American black boy," he shouted angrily, staring straight into Darryl's eyes. "I could blow you away and nobody would ever know."

Darryl looked back unflinchingly into Al's eyes.

"I wouldn't recommend that," Darryl said. "If I were you—"

"What?" Al replied angrily.

"I know where that other half ton of weed is hidden in the woods of South Georgia," Darryl said. "And you don't."

Al grimaced as he reconsidered. He glanced thoughtfully from J.L. to Karina and then back to Darryl. Finally, he released Darryl's shirt and called him to the side. Darryl followed Al some distance from the others so they could talk privately. J.L. and Karina watched as Al spoke anxiously to Darryl, pointed in the distance, and whispered orders. Once Al was finished talking, Darryl returned to J.L. and Karina.

"He's going to give y'all a fair chance," Darryl said. "Do you see that cow fence on the other side of this pasture?"

J.L. peered into the distance.

"I see it," he said.

"Okay, Darryl continued. "You two take your suitcases

and slowly walk across the field to that fence. Slowly cross the fence. Once you are on the other side, start running as fast as you can."

"Why?" Karina asked.

"Because Al and his boys will be shooting at you."

"Oh God! Oh God!" Karina pleaded. "Don't shoot us! Please don't shoot us!"

"And when you start running," Daryl continued, "be sure you run toward that highway over there. If you run the other direction, you'll be dead for sure."

"Oh, we'll run in the right direction," J.L. said. "You can count on it!"

"Okay," Darryl ordered. "Go! Go!"

With that, J.L. and Karina, suitcases in hand, started walking across the pasture.

"Oh, please don't shoot us!" Karina pleaded as they walked. "Oh, please don't shoot us!"

Several minutes later, they reached the fence. J.L. threw his suitcase over the fence and then threw Karina's over. He climbed over the fence and helped Karina. The moment they were on the other side of the fence, both of them grabbed their suitcases and started running.

"Run!" J.L. shouted. "Run for your life!"

In a flash, they were running full speed down the dirt road.

Behind them, they could hear shots from the pistols of Al and his men. Several shots rang out as J.L. and Karina ran down the road. Finally, the shooting stopped.

J.L. looked behind them. They were at least three hundred yards from the scene of the airplane.

"Let's rest for a minute," J.L. said, falling into the short grass along the roadside and gasping for breath. Karina collapsed breathlessly on the grass beside him.

Almost Home

After they had caught their breath, J.L. stood up, reached down his hand, and pulled her to her feet.

"Come on!" he said. "Let's walk up to the highway."

About ten minutes later, they arrived at the highway and Karina recognized it immediately.

"That's Highway 44," Karina said excitedly. "We're only about fifteen miles from Port Everglades."

J.L. peered into the distance. "Look," he said. "There's a bus station. This is our lucky day. Come on!"

***

Twenty minutes later, they were standing in line at the bus station, waiting to buy a ticket. As he stood in line, he watched as the person ahead of him bought a ticket with a credit card. The clerk swiped the credit card and then asked him to enter his pin. The customer entered the pin, the printer started clicking, and the machine spit out a ticket. The customer took the ticket and left the counter.

"Oh, hell," J.L. said with dread in his voice. "Here we go again with another fricking computer."

"I'm keeping my fingers crossed," she said.

"If it doesn't work, we may be walking these last few miles," he said.

J.L. approached the counter. The clerk was an unsmiling middle-aged woman with dark hair. "Can I help you?" she greeted.

"Are your computers working?" J.L. asked.

"Of course," she replied.

"We want to get two tickets to Port Everglades."

The woman started punching keys on the computer keyboard. J.L. looked warily at Karina and she returned the look.

"That will be $28.50," the clerk said.

J.L. handed her the credit card.

She swiped it. "Enter your pin," she said.

J.L. entered the last four numbers of his social security number and a new screen appeared.

"Do you want cash back?" the clerk asked.

"I can get cash back?" J.L. said.

"Sure," the clerk said.

"Can I get one hundred dollars?"

With that, the clerk punched more buttons. Instantly, the machine started digesting the entered data and the printer spit out two bus tickets.

The clerk handed the tickets and cash to J.L. He took the cash and tickets and then he and Karina burst out laughing. The clerk was not amused.

"Did I say something funny?" she asked.

"Oh no," he said. "I'm sorry. Thanks for your help."

"The waiting room is to the right," the clerk said. "You can buy food and drinks from the machines."

***

Thirty minutes later, J.L. and Karina were cruising south down Highway 44. Both were staring out of the bus window, eating chicken salad sandwiches and watching the Florida countryside fly past.

"Oh God, cowboy," she said. "We're going to make it. We're really going to make it. I would never have believed it. After all we've been through, we're going to make it."

"We were supposed to make it," J.L. said. "We're good people. We deserve to make it. My daddy used to say, 'Always keep your karma clean because good things only come to people who deserve it.'"

She looked wistfully at him.

"Will you hold me for a minute?"

He put his arm around her and held her tightly to his chest. Finally, J.L. spoke up.

"Do you remember what you said back there on the plane

when you thought we were going to die?" he asked.

"I remember."

"Did you mean it?"

She looked at him.

"Yes," she replied. "I've fallen in love with you during all of this."

J.L. didn't reply.

"Do you have romantic feelings for me?" she asked.

"I'd be a liar if I said I hadn't thought about it," he said. "I have to admit I've grown very fond of you over the past eight days."

They rode silently.

"Can I kiss you?" he asked.

"You don't have to ask," she said, reaching up and cupping his face in her hands and kissing him softly on the lips. For a long moment, they held the kiss.

Suddenly, they heard a disapproving cough across the aisle. A middle-aged fat man, who had been reading a newspaper, was peering at them.

"We're being watched," J.L. said, breaking the embrace.

They rode quietly for several minutes. Both were staring out the bus window.

Finally, he turned and looked at her. She sensed his gaze and turned to meet his eyes.

"Why are you looking at me like that?" she asked.

"Why are you looking at me like that?" he replied.

He turned back to the window.

"We'll be there in a few minutes," she said. "Why don't you stay a while with me at Rancho Escobar?"

"I can't miss that boat," he said. "It leaves tomorrow at noon."

"I know," she said. "Tell you what, if you'll spend some time with me, I'll get somebody to take you to Miami. It's only about thirty minutes away."

"Who will take me?"

"The caretaker."

He looked at her.

"I want to show you the ranch," she added.
"Okay," he said. "I've got some time."

Rancho Escobar

Port Everglades, Florida, was a small, migrant-settled, agricultural hamlet located ten miles north of the Big Cypress National Swamp Reserve along Florida's west coast, a primal land of alligators, cypress trees, mangroves, and seemingly mile upon endless mile of brackish, reed-filled water. The little town was built with the sweat, blood, and tears of the weary souls who came from other nations—especially Mexico, Central America, and the Caribbean—to get a shot at the American dream. These dreams were to be borne out of what meager existence they could glean from planting and harvesting sugar cane and citrus crops and tending livestock on the ranches of inland Florida. It was a town inhabited and settled by cane cutters, citrus grove workers, and cowboys.

J.L. and Karina, suitcases in hand, walked down the little town's main street.

"Things haven't changed much in twelve years," she said, observing the town's buildings. "They got a new post office up where the fire station used to be, and they've added a small church on the corner over there."

"Interesting little town," J.L. said, stopping momentarily to peek inside a carnicería. "I'd forgotten how much I loved Latin things."

She looked over distractedly at J.L. "Come on, cowboy," she said. "We'll walk down Main to Fourth Street and go right. The ranchito is about four blocks."

They continued walking past a taco shop, a natural gas company, a hardware store, a citrus fruit-packing house, and the sheriff's office. J.L glanced up at the sheriff's office. The sign on the glass window read: Lester Smallwoods, Everglades County Sheriff. He peeked inside the window and saw an overweight uniformed officer with his feet propped up on a desk, watching a small television. He walked on, following her lead.

Moments later, they turned the corner off Main to Fourth Street. Immediately after turning the corner, they saw railroad tracks, which served the citrus-packing houses that fronted on the town's main street.

"These are the tracks for the Florida Central Railroad," Karina said. "The train comes by every night at six to load up the produce and take it to Miami. When I was a little girl, I would lie in bed and wait for the train to arrive before I would go to sleep. On a quiet night, I could hear the whistle from as far away as Fort Myers. I've always loved trains."

"I love trains too," J.L. said. "More than any other single mode of transportation, they settled the West. Horses were for short-distance transportation, but it was trains that took people long distances."

Some ten minutes later, they were out of the downtown area.

"See all of that," she said, pointing to the thick swamp foliage and the wetlands beyond. "When I lived with Aunt Lydia, my cousin Julio and I would ride horses across those fields and into the swamps. I know those swamps and wetlands like the back of my hand."

"Boy, all this sure is pretty," he said. "I've never seen all this up close before. I've seen pictures in books, but never seen it in real life."

He picked up a handful of the white sand and threw it into the air.

"That's the finest sand I've ever seen," he said. "The grains are as fine as sugar."

They walked quietly, suitcases in hand.

"When I was twelve or thirteen years old," Karina said finally, "my aunt would send me down this road to town to buy bread and coffee. Some days, as I walked to the store, I would see this weird man who went from house to house selling combs. He would walk along the road saying, 'Vendo pienes baratos! Vendo pienes baratos!' I sell cheap combs! I sell cheap combs!" He was tall and had a deep voice. Every time I would see him, the hair on my neck would rise and I would run off into the bushes and hide until he passed."

J.L. looked at her. "You've spent a lot of time running, haven't you?" he asked.

"Yeah, I guess I have," she said. "You've spent some time running yourself."

He looked at her and smiled. "Yeah, I have," he replied.

"Look, look!" she shouted with excitement. "There's the portal." Suitcase in hand, she broke into a full run and raced the final yards to the ranch entrance.

"Wait for me," he said, hurrying his gait to catch up to her.

Moments later, they were standing in front of the main entrance to an old Spanish-style ranch. The entrance was a concrete and brick structure with a metal gate. Over the entrance was a dust-covered, terra-cotta-lettered marquee that had once read "Rancho Escobar." The letter "s" had fallen from its position in the marquee.

J.L. picked up the "s" and blew off the dust.

"This was once a working spread," J.L. said. "I didn't know you were inheriting a real ranch..."

"Oh, yes," Karina replied. "Some of the happiest days of my life were spent here."

As they peered toward the ranch's main house, a man walked across the courtyard toward an old pickup truck.

Immediately, Karina stepped to the gate.

"Raul! Raul!" she called.

The man looked up.

He peered toward the entrance for a moment, then took off his hat and waved it in greeting.

"Karina! Karina!" he called.

Then he turned and started walking down the road leading to the entrance.

"Come on!" she said. "I want you to meet Raul. He's the ranch caretaker."

Instantly, she opened the gate and, suitcase in hand, started running down the road to meet the man. J.L. watched as she rushed up happily and hugged the man. Then, holding his hand, she led him back to meet J.L.

Raul Sanchez was a medium-built Cuban man in his early sixties. Dressed in rough workman's clothes, he had a heavy gray mustache and a weather-beaten face.

"Cowboy, this is Raul," she said.

J.L. smiled and shook the man's hand.

Raul pointed from Karina to J.L. "You two are...?" he asked, wondering whether they were a couple.

"Oh no!" she said quickly. "We're just good friends."

She turned to J.L. "Come on, cowboy," she said. "I've got some things I want to show you."

***

Moments later, they were standing in the courtyard of the main house. Built in the style of old California rancheros, it was a stucco, terra-cotta-colored, two-story structure with rooms built around a central courtyard and a fountain in the center. The once-proud courtyard had fallen into severe disrepair. Tall weeds had grown up between the courtyard tiles. The old ceramic fountain had seen no water in many years and its adornments—birds, flowers, and a smiling sun— had crumbled away with age and weather. Beyond the house, there was an aging barn and dilapidated outbuildings for livestock. The entire ranch was surrounded with densely over-grown pastures enclosed by an aging, rotting rail fence. From all indications, the grounds had once been a thriving, working ranch, but now had fallen into disrepair with age and neglect.

"What happened?" Karina asked. "When I was here twelve years ago, this place was a working ranch. There were horses and cattle and wranglers and tack. This is all that's left?"

Raul nodded his head sadly. "After your aunt's health took a turn for the worse, she didn't have the will or the money to keep it going."

"Yes, I know," Karina said sadly. "In her letters, I could sense she had lost interest in the place. The illness was taking a terrible toll."

"Cattle feed kept getting higher and higher," Raul continued. "There were labor costs and repair bills and fuel bills and, finally, she let the hired hands go and sold the cattle. It was too much for her."

Karina didn't reply at first.

"Well, cowboy," she lamented, turning to J.L. "Don't tell me about dreams again. They can die just as fast as they are born."

J.L. looked at her and said nothing.

Karina shook her head in abject disappointment.

"Come on," she said. "I'll show you my old room."

Once inside the ranch's main house, J.L. could see that the house was well appointed for its day. There were finely finished terrazzo floors and intricately carved window frames and massive exposed beams across the ceiling. Karina led them up the stairs and stopped in front of one bedroom. Before opening the door, she turned to J.L.

"I lived in this room for three years," she said.

She opened the door and they stepped inside. There was a musty, long-unkempt smell and a thin layer of dust on all of the furnishings. The bed was a huge, Spanish-style, Old World model with an ornate metal headboard and matching dresser. Throughout the room, there were childhood photos of her with Aunt Lydia, her mother, father, cousins, and other family members. There were ribbons for horse shows, a high school diploma, and other assorted childhood memorabilia.

"It's just the way I left it twelve years ago," Karina said.

"That's the way your aunt wanted it," Raul said. "Many times, she would say she wanted to come up here and find you asleep. She loved you so much."

She noted a small green cap hanging on a nail next to the bed. "There's my old Campfire Girls cap," she said.

She took it from the nail and examined it and then she brushed off the dust and put it on her head. For a moment, she studied the image.

"Do I look thirteen again?" she asked, looking at Raul.

"Oh, Karina," he said with a sly smile. "You look much

younger than that. You're still as beautiful as you were then."

She smiled. "And you are such a wonderful liar!" she said, removing the cap and replacing it on the nail.

She turned and walked out of the room and J.L. and Raul followed her out. In the kitchen, Karina, caught up in a flood of old memories, pointed out an old hacienda-style, wood-burning cook stove.

"Many days, I sat at the table there, playing and watching Aunt Lydia cooking at the stove. Even now, I can smell the red peppers and garlic and cilantro she would mix into her dishes."

She sighed at the lost memories and then turned and headed to the back door as J.L. and Raul followed. In the back yard, they followed a concrete walkway surrounded by knee-high grass that led from the ranch's back entrance to the barn. Under a tree, she saw an old pickup truck.

"That's Uncle Albert's old pickup," she said. "Does it still run?"

"Oh yes," Raul said. "I still haul hay in it. The key is in the kitchen over the sink where it's always been."

They continued walking.

She looked out to the pasture beyond and saw a single horse grazing peacefully.

"Oh my God!" she said, turning to Raul. "Is that Mariah?"

Raul nodded with a smile.

"She's fifteen years old now," he said. "Your aunt wouldn't sell her. She said she wanted Mariah to die and be buried on the ranch. She's the only livestock left here."

Karina turned and raced to the fence, then pulled herself to the top rail.

"Mariah! Mariah!" she called.

Instantly, the horse instinctively looked up toward the sound of her voice. The horse whinnied quietly, threw its head into the air, and galloped across the field to Karina. At the fence, some ten feet from her, the horse broke the gallop, went into a walk, and slowly ambled up to her as if greeting an old friend.

"Oh my God!" she said. "After all these years, she still knows me."

Her eyes filled with tears as the horse leaned its head over the top rail.

"Sweet, sweet Mariah," she said, holding her head to the horse's head and stroking its forehead. Then, overcome with emotion, she stopped and buried her face in her hands.

"Karina!" Raul asked sympathetically. "What's wrong?"

"I'm just so happy to be home," she said, wiping away tears. "I'd forgotten how much I loved this place."

Finally, she dried her eyes.

"I'm sorry," she said, looking up apologetically at Raul and J.L. They started walking back toward the main house.

"Okay," Raul said hesitantly. "You've got to hear the bad news sooner or later."

"Yeah, I know," she said. "Go ahead and tell me."

"The state is going to put the ranch up for sale if the back taxes aren't paid by January of next year."

"How much is owed?" Karina asked.

"It's a lot," Raul said. "I don't know for sure," he said. "You'll have to talk to the lawyer about that."

"Oh God," Karina said. "I would hate to see this place go to the state for taxes. Aunt Lydia loved this ranch. She and Uncle Albert put their whole lives into this place."

"I know," Raul said sadly. "Only too well do I know that. Are you going to be staying here?"

"Yes," she said. "I don't have anywhere else to go."

"I hope you can save it," Raul said. "If you can't save it, I'll have to find a new place to live."

"I'm going to do my best," she said. "If I stay here, you can stay here. That's a promise."

"Oh, thanks," he said. "I've got to go into Port Everglades to buy some things."

"I understand," she said.

Raul turned to J.L.

"A pleasure to meet you," Raul said, offering his hand to J.L.

Karina and J.L. watched as Raul strode across the yard, got into the old pickup, and, in a cloud of dust, headed back down the roadway to the ranch entrance.

"Come on," she said. "Let's walk down to the cattle lane."

Romance

The cattle lane was a narrow barbed-wire-fenced passageway through which cattle would pass as they moved from the pasture to the barn. Although it had become heavily overgrown with dense undergrowth, J.L. and Karina could still find traces of the old pathway.

"I can't believe how beautiful all this is," J.L. said, marveling at the lush, green surroundings. "This place is like paradise. I just love all of this."

They walked along the lane until they reached a child's swing that had been built under a giant Florida oak tree.

"Come on," she said. "I want you to push me in the swing."

J.L. held his foot on the lower strand of barbed wire and pulled the higher strand upward to create an opening in the fence for her to pass through. As she ducked through the opening, she ripped a huge tear in the right side of her top.

"You tore your top," he observed, passing through the fence.

She looked down at the tear, which had exposed most of the brassiere over her right breast. She playfully flipped the torn piece dangling from her top.

"It doesn't matter," she said with a smile. "Come swing me."

As he helped her into the swing, she reminisced, "I've always loved this swing. When I was a child, I would come here to be alone. It was the one place where I could find peace."

Moments later, J.L. was pushing her in the swing while a light, misting rain fell.

"Higher!" she said, her long black hair flying in the breeze as she swung up and down. As the swing returned, he pushed her even higher.

"Wheeeeeee!" she said delightedly as the swing's arc took her higher and higher.

J.L. turned distractedly from the swing and peered across the pastures to the line of cypress trees and the wetlands beyond. "God, I love this place," he said. "It's so green and rich and verdant."

She laughed. "It's so what? What is 'verdant'?"

"You know," he said, "rich and green and filled with life."

Karina started dragging her feet with each successive arc and, finally, the tire swing came to a halt.

J.L. looked over at her as the misting rain grew thicker.

She was watching him as he peered across the pastures.

"You don't want to swing me anymore?"

Saying nothing, he walked back to the swing and faced her.

She looked up at him. Her face was moist from the rain. He put his hands on her shoulders and then slowly brought them up to her neck and held her face. She didn't move and peered softly, submissively into his eyes. He leaned his face down to hers and kissed her tenderly on the lips.

"Your face is wet," he said matter-of-factly.

She smiled and continued peering into his face.

"So is yours," she replied softly.

He looked down at the rip in her top and peered at her bosom.

"Rain is running down your chest and onto your breasts," he said, reaching his hand into her bosom.

She smiled happily, pulling her arms in to hold his hand tightly against her breast. He leaned forward and kissed her gently again.

As they held the kiss, the rain began pouring down in gigantic watery splooshes. He broke the kiss and removed his hand.

"Come on," he said. "Let's get out of this rain."

He helped her out of the swing and, together, hand in hand, they ducked back through the barbed wire fence and raced back down the cattle lane to the barn.

Moments later, they were standing in the barn hallway, watching the spring rain come down in giant torrents.

"I love rain," she said. "There's something very personal about rain." She looked up at him. "You know I've become very fond of you," she said.

"Yes," he replied. "And I've become very fond of you." He put his hands on her waist and pulled her to him. "You said in Memphis you weren't saving it for anybody," he said matter-of-factly.

"I offered in Atlanta," she said. "And you pushed me away."

"I'm accepting this time," he said. "How do you want to do it?"

"Do what?" she asked coyly.

"You know."

She smiled. "We can go to my old room," she said. "It's been a million years since I've been on that bed."

"We're going to get wet."

She looked out at the pouring rain and nodded her agreement.

"How do you want to do it?" she asked.

"Isn't there a hayloft above us?"

"Yes," she replied. "I'll get some horse blankets from the tack room."

Moments later, they were up the ladder and into the hayloft. Together, they spread out the horse blankets on the soft, loose hay while the rain pounded on the barn's tin roof.

Quickly, she removed her clothing. Just as quickly, he was naked.

"Come on," he said, holding out his arms and inviting her into his naked body.

"I hope you like me," she said.

***

Twenty minutes later, they lay naked on the horse blankets

in the loose hay. Both were breathing heavily and the air was thick with the smell of fresh rain, new-mown hay, and passionate sex. He looked at her and her naked body on the horse blanket. He realized it was one of the most beautiful things he'd ever seen.

"You have a lot of good moves," he said. "I like that."

"You've got some pretty good moves yourself, J.L." she said.

J.L. looked at her.

"J.L.?" he asked. "That's the first time you've called me J.L."

"I've just made passionate love with you," she said. "I can't refer to you as plain old 'cowboy' after that."

He laughed.

"Will you tell me what the J.L. stands for now?" she said. "Do I know you well enough now?"

He smiled.

"Will you promise not to laugh?"

"I promise," she said.

"Jerome Lafayette."

She burst out laughing, her breasts and entire body shaking with laughter.

"You promised not to laugh."

"I'm not laughing because the name is ridiculous," she said. "I'm laughing because you're so ashamed of it. That's a great name."

"Really? You really think so?"

""Yes, I think it's a great name."

They grew silent.

J.L. stood up in his nakedness, turned from her, and walked across the floor to the loft's outside opening. For a moment, he stood peering out at the pouring rain. Then, he turned and looked back at her. She got up and came to his side and they stood together in their nakedness, peering out at the rain.

"I've fallen in love with you," she said. "I've learned so much about you and who you are in the past few days. You're the most decent man I've ever known."

"I've never thought of myself as being decent, as such," he said. "I just always tried to do the right thing."

She didn't reply.

"I've learned a lot about you too," he said finally. "We've had lots of karma together in the past few days."

She put her arm around his naked waist and pulled him to her. With their naked bodies touching front-to-front, she looked into his eyes.

"So what are you going to do?" she asked.

He didn't answer. For a long moment, he looked into her eyes and then he removed her hands from his body and returned to the horse blankets. She followed him.

"I've got to get on this ship," he said finally. "My whole life is planned around the trip to Argentina."

"You could stay here," she said. "We could get this ranch up and running again; we could rebuild it. You know all about horses and cattle and ranching."

He looked at her.

"It's tempting," he said. "Very tempting, but my whole life has been planned around this trip to Argentina. I can't go changing horses in the middle of the stream."

She didn't answer at first. "I want to be with you, J.L.," she said.

He looked at her. "Why don't you come to Argentina with me?" he asked. "I've got two tickets. They'll feed us on the boat. We'll have our own cabin and I'll have a job when we get there."

"I could never leave the USA," she said.

There was a long pause.

"What's more, I want to be married," she said. "I want a ring and a commitment and an assurance that the man I'm going to love is mine and mine alone."

Another long pause.

"As much as I like you, I'm not sure I could get married again."

"Why not?"

"I'm afraid."

"Afraid of what?"

"I'm just not ready to turn my emotions loose with a woman again," he said. "Love can be wonderful, but it also causes a lot of heartache."

She knew he was right. She shook her head disappointedly.

"Don't get me wrong," he continued. "I've grown very fond of you. I've learned to respect you and appreciate you."

"Have you learned to love me?"

"I don't know how to answer that," he said. "In my heart, I'm not sure I could handle the responsibility of love and marriage again."

She looked at him. "I'm tired of running," she said. "I want to settle down."

"I get that feeling myself sometimes," he said, "but I'm just not sure that I'm ready yet. I love my freedom too much. At the moment, my plans are to get on that ship and go to Argentina."

"What would it take to get you to settle down?"

"I'm not sure," he said. "I just feel that I'm not ready yet."

She looked at him, knowing she was getting nowhere.

Okay," she said finally, "We've got work to do."

"What?"

"The agreement was that if you get me to Port Everglades, I would help you get to Miami and onto that ship."

"You don't have to do that," he said.

"But I want to," she replied. "It was part of the deal."

"You can go to the bus station with me," he said. "I'll be fine on the ride to Miami."

"Come on," she said. "I'll go with you to the bus station."

Jailbreak

J.L., suitcase in hand, and Karina walked quietly back down Main Street to the bus station. As they approached the sheriff's office, they could see the sheriff, a fiftyish man with a big gut and bifocals, sitting out front in a rocking chair, reading a newspaper.

"Can you carry my suitcase while I open a pack of gum?" he asked.

"Sure," she said, taking the suitcase.

J.L. opened the pack of gum.

"Want a piece?" he asked.

"No, thanks," she said.

J.L. unwrapped the stick of gum and threw the wrapper toward a waste can in front of the sheriff's office and missed. They walked on past, but the sheriff's deputy looked up and saw that the wrapper had missed its mark.

"Hey, mister," the sheriff called to J.L.

"Yes, sir?"

"Your chewing gum wrapper missed the trashcan."

"The street sweeper will get that," J.L. said, smiling.

"We ain't got no street sweeper," he said. "Come over and pick this up."

J.L. hesitated.

"If you don't, I'll charge you with littering," the sheriff said.

"Oh, okay," J.L. said.

He walked back, picked up the wrapper, gently placed it in the trashcan, and then turned to the sheriff. "Are we happy now?" J.L. asked.

The deputy jumped angrily out of the rocking chair.

"Look, mister, we don't like smart guys around here," he

said. "You got ID?"

"Yes, sir."

"Let me see it!"

J.L. reached for his billfold and produced the Washington state driver's license.

The sheriff examined it.

"Jerome L. Crockett, C/O of the Lazy B Ranch, Lonesome Trail Road, Spokane, Washington," he read aloud.

The sheriff examined the photo and compared the likeness.

"Come inside with me," he ordered.

J.L. shrugged his shoulders and started inside.

Karina started in with them.

"You stay out here," the sheriff said, turning to Karina.

The sheriff stopped and examined her closely.

"Aren't you Lydia Escobar's daughter?"

"I'm her niece."

"I thought I recognized you," he said. "Where were y'all going?"

"To the bus station."

"Whose suitcase is that?" the sheriff asked, reaching for it.

"It's mine," she said quickly, jerking it back.

The sheriff turned back to J.L.

"Okay," he said. "You stay out here. Me and him are going inside."

Moments later, inside the office, J.L. watched as the sheriff, seated in front of a computer, typed in data. After a few seconds, he stopped, punched a key, went to the printer, and then grabbed a sheet of paper. He examined the paper and then turned to J.L.

"This warrant here says you're a fugitive from justice in Illinois," he said. "You're wanted for murder and armed robbery."

"That's not me," J.L. said. "That's another J.L. Crockett."

"Until I know that for sure, you're under arrest," the sheriff said.

"Wait," J.L. said. "A policeman told me that in South Dakota—"

"Tell it to the judge," the sheriff said, clasping J.L.'s hands behind his back and applying handcuffs. "Come on; you're going to jail."

Karina burst into the office. "What are you doing?" she screamed angrily.

"This man is under arrest," the sheriff said.

"Are you crazy?" she screamed. "For what?"

"Murder and armed robbery."

"This man wouldn't hurt a flea," she protested angrily.

"He's going to jail right now," the sheriff said. "Now if you're smart, you'll get out of here."

"Holy Christ!" she shouted. "You call yourself law and order. You question him for littering and then you arrest him for murder and armed robbery?"

"Get out of here or you'll be going with him," the sheriff ordered.

She glared angrily at the sheriff and then stormed out the door.

***

Two hours later, J.L. was sitting dejectedly on a bunk in the Everglades County jail. The jail cell was a narrow, gray-walled affair with two steel bunk beds, a commode, and a heavily barred rear window to the outside world. On the bunk opposite him, a drunk was talking deliriously.

"Oh, it was her eyes," the drunk was saying. "I always remember those eyes. She had cold black eyes like some demon from hell and when you looked into them, you could see all eternity. And her breasts, they were as white and beautiful as freshly driven snow."

The drunk fell silent and drifted off to sleep.

The air was thick with the smell of citrus fruit.

J.L. stepped away from the bunk and looked outside. Through the bars, he could see the railroad tracks. At the packinghouse on the opposite side of the tracks, he could see stacked crates of oranges, grapefruit, and limes on a loading dock, waiting to be shipped on the next train. For a moment, he relished the citrus smell.

"Oh, you would have loved Bill," the drunk mumbled. "He was quite a man. Tall, good-looking guy, well spoken, and boy, did he have a way with the girls. He could get all of them—redheads, blondes, brunettes. I'll tell you, Billy was quite a ladies' man."

J.L. heard rapping on the bars. He turned and saw a deputy outside the cell.

"J.L. Crockett?"

"That's me."

"You've got a visitor," he said.

***

Moments later, the deputy led J.L. into a small enclosed holding cell. He could see Karina waiting outside.

"You've got ten minutes," the deputy said. "Keep the conversation loud enough that I can hear what you're saying. No whispering. I'll be right over here."

With that, the deputy turned and seated himself nearby and started reading a newspaper.

"I told my sister that you were a good person, and she said she believed that also."

J.L. looked at her quizzically, not understanding.

"She said she would take all of your washing and get it back to you on Friday. She promised to put light starch in all of your shirts and iron them just the way you like them."

A phone rang.

"I've got to go answer the phone," the deputy said sternly. "No funny stuff, okay?"

The deputy left the desk, went to the other office, and started talking on the phone.

"What are you doing?" he asked.

"I'm going to get you out of here," she said.

"What?" he asked incredulously. "How are you going to do that?"

"Just let me handle it," she said confidently. "Be ready at six."

J.L. couldn't believe what he was hearing.

"Why are you doing this?" he asked.

"Because I love you," she said. "I want to see you on that boat."

J.L. glanced over at the deputy and saw that he had finished on the phone and was returning to the nearby desk.

"The deputy is coming back," J.L. said.

"Be ready at six," she said again.

***

An hour later, J.L. was pacing the cell floor. The drunk was sound asleep and snoring loudly. He glanced up at the clock in the jail's front office. It was 5:56 p.m. Through the barred window at the rear of the jail, he could see workers with forklifts loading palettes of citrus fruit onto the train. Finally, all of the palettes were loaded and J.L. watched as the workers slammed and locked each of the train car doors. He watched as one worker looked toward the front of the train and signaled to the engineer that the train was loaded and ready to go. At the worker's signal, the train's engine groaned and strained as the train started pulling away from the loading dock.

J.L. heard a strange sound coming from the window as if it were about to be rent asunder. Then, as he watched, the cell window buckled outward and, with a loud crash, the cell window and part of the wall fell away, leaving a gaping hole in the back wall of the jail.

The loud sound woke up the drunk.

"Oh great God, he's here! He's here!" the drunk said deliriously. "Bill's come back for me."

For a moment, the entire cell was filled with concrete dust. J.L. started coughing and waving his hand so he could see through the dust. Then, as the dust cleared, he peered through the hole in the cell wall at the outside world and saw Karina astride the mare at the back of the jail.

"Come on!" she yelled frantically. "Come on!"

Quickly, J.L. stepped through the hole in the side of the jail wall and sprinted to Karina and the waiting mare. He grabbed the saddle horn and swung up in the saddle behind her. Once he was in the saddle, the mare lunged forward and was instantly in a full gallop. As the mare galloped away, J.L. looked back and could see that one end of a rope had been tied to the cell bars and another had been tied to the train. The forward force of the moving train had pulled the barred window and part of the wall out of the Everglades County jail.

Karina, astride the mare with J.L. riding double, streaked across the field behind the jail. The mare was swift and sure of foot as they raced back to Rancho Escobar. Back at the ranch, the mare galloped swiftly down the road past the main house and into the barn. They dismounted and she quickly unsaddled the horse.

"Your suitcase is already in the truck," she said, pointing to her uncle's old pickup they had seen earlier in the yard. "We're going to Miami in that."

Dogs, Bogs, and Logs

Twenty minutes later, the old pickup was speeding south down Highway 141 toward Alligator Alley. Karina was at the wheel with J.L. in the passenger seat and his suitcase between them. It was 6:22.

"If we don't hit much traffic, we should be in Miami in about thirty minutes," she said.

Ten minutes later, the truck pulled to a stop behind a slow moving line of traffic.

"I wonder why these cars are backed up," she said. "There must be a wreck."

For several minutes, they waited patiently as the line of cars slowly inched forward. Finally, after they rounded a curve, Karina could see the flashing blue lights of a sheriff's car just ahead of them.

"The sheriff's set up a roadblock," she said.

"What are we going to do now?" J.L. asked.

She looked at him.

"Do you see the hole in the park fence?" she asked, pointing to the right side of the road at the tornado link fence that bordered the highway.

J.L. peered along the side of the road. "I see it," he said.

"Grab your suitcase," she said. "We're going into the swamps."

"Are you crazy?"

"You want to go back to jail and miss the boat?"

He looked at her. "I see what you mean," he said. He grabbed the suitcase.

"On three," she said. "One, two, three—go!"

Instantly, the two of them were out of the pickup truck and headed for the hole in the park fence.

As they ducked under the park fence, they heard the sheriff yell.

"There they are!" he shouted, pointing them out to two nearby deputies. "They're going into the swamps! Get the dogs!"

"Sheriff, we can't go in there," the deputy said. "That's federal property."

"Get the dogs!" the sheriff ordered again.

The deputy looked curiously at the sheriff.

"Now!" he shouted. "Get the dogs and get them now!"

The deputy turned and started back to his squad car to the radio.

***

Five minutes later, J.L., suitcase in hand, and Karina, were running frantically along a sandy, horse-made trail somewhere in the Big Cypress National Reserve. On either side, the trail was dense with low-standing palmetto bushes and Florida scrub pines.

"Let's stop for a minute," she said breathlessly.

They stopped, both trying to catch their breath.

Behind them, they heard the barking of a bloodhound.

"Hear that?" J.L. said. "He's about five hundred yards back. Come on!"

They started running again. About fifty yards further down the trail, J.L. spotted a fork in the path.

"Stop!" he said. "Take off your shoes!"

"What?" she asked.

"Take off your shoes," he replied, sitting on his suitcase and unlacing his shoes. "I'm going to try to throw off that dog."

After their shoes were removed, J.L. broke a long branch from a nearby tree and tied the shoes to one end of the branch. Then, standing inside the fork in the trail, he dragged the shoes back and forth along the opposite fork.

"That should do it," he said.

They put their shoes back on and started running down the

trail.

Moments later, they heard the dog again.

The barking was coming from further away, from the fork in the trail.

"It worked," J.L. said. "That'll give us a little time."

***

Over the next fifteen minutes, they raced together down the sandy trail. Finally, they stopped. The trail had vanished into the thick foliage of a swamp jungle made up of cypress trees, air plants, and undergrowth. They stood together, trying to catch their breath.

"We can't go in there," he said. "We'll get lost and never find our way out."

"Wait!" Karina said. "I know this place. Me and Julio used to play here when we were children."

She turned from J.L. and walked some distance back up the trail, trying to get her bearings and see some detail she recognized. J.L. followed.

"That's Kitchen's Creek," she said, pointing to the tree line in the distance. "I thought I recognized this place. There is a narrow place in the creek up there where hunters used to place a foot log to get across the creek. Come on!"

She started through the thick, green undergrowth along the tree line. J.L. followed. Moments later, they picked up another faint trail. For about twenty minutes, they trekked through the thick undergrowth along the banks of the creek. Finally, Karin stopped and looked ahead.

"This is it!" Karina said. "The foot log should be right up here."

Behind them, they could hear the barking of bloodhounds.

Moments later, they reached a narrow point in the creek and they could see a distinct trail through a cypress grove that led to a foot log across the creek. The barking was getting nearer.

At the foot log, J.L. stopped.

"Let me test it first," he said, stomping his foot on the log to test its strength. "We don't want to go into that water."

"Remember, I can't swim," she said.

J.L. looked at her. Then, he mounted the log to test it further.

"It seems strong enough," he said. "I'm going across. Do you want me to help you?"

"No, I'll be fine," she replied.

Moments later, J.L. was across the foot log and on the other side of the creek.

"Just be careful!" he said.

"Let me have your suitcase!" she said. "I can balance myself with it."

He walked across the log, handed his suitcase to her, and then went back across the log. Karina started across the foot log.

"Just stay calm," J.L. said, watching her.

Holding the suitcase in one hand and holding out her other arm to balance herself, she walked across the log. Safe on the other side, she handed him the suitcase.

"Come on!" she said. "There used to be an old park ranger's shack not far from here."

"No, wait!" J.L. said, taking his suitcase from her.

"What are you doing?" she asked.

"That dog has got to cross this log too," he replied. "Let's wait for him."

Moments later, as predicted, the lead dog appeared on the opposite site of the creek, barking ferociously at J.L. and Karina. Then, the dog spotted the foot log. For a moment, the animal cautiously approached the log and then, confident that the log was safe, started across to the other side of the creek. Once the dog was midway across the log, J.L. slammed his suitcase into the log. The sudden jolt caused the dog to lose his balance and, with a helpless yelp, the dog fell into the creek. As J.L. and Karina watched, the dog was swimming for dear life as the swift-moving water carried the animal rapidly downstream. Moments later, the dog, still swimming, disappeared around a bend in the creek.

J.L. hefted the end of the small log on his side of the creek and threw it into the water. They watched as the current carried the small log down the stream.

"Now we've got some time," J.L. said.

"Let's find the old ranger's shack," she said. "If we can get through the night, I know a back route to the ranch. It's about two miles, but we can make it."

Twenty minutes later, they were tromping through a waist-high field of low-standing palmetto intermixed with broom sage and saw grass. Years of forest ranger vehicle use had created two narrow slits through the sea of waist-high swamp vegetation. In the west, J.L. could see that the sun was setting.

"It will be dark before long," he said.

"Look, there it is!" she said.

Moments later, they stood in front of a twelve-foot-by-twelve-foot tin shack. Inside, they found a small metal desk and a connection for a telephone. On the back wall was a map of the shack's exact location in the Everglades National Forest.

"I wonder if there's any food around here," J.L. said, rummaging through the desk drawers. "Look at this," he said, pulling out a box of granola bars.

He opened one of the bars and took a bite.

"Old," he said, "but edible."

He handed her one.

"No," she said, shaking her head. "I'm tired. I've got to rest."

She slumped on the floor and was soon sound asleep.

Dead End

Seven hours later, inside the ranger's shack, J.L. and Karina were sound asleep. J.L. was dreaming about the 2002 Rodeo Championships in Oklahoma City in which he had competed, when he was awakened by the raucous barking of dogs. Through the crack in the door, he could see several flashlights beaming inside.

Suddenly, Karina sprang wide awake and looked frantically at J.L.

"Oh God," she said desperately. "They've got us! There's nowhere for us to run now."

J.L. nodded. Then, there was a sharp rap on the side of the tin building.

"Come out with your hands up!" a deputy shouted. "Come out or we'll start shooting."

"We're coming out!" J.L. shouted. "We're coming out! Don't shoot!"

J.L. unlatched the door and, together, hands held high, they emerged from the tin shack.

In the darkness, they could see four flashlight beams shining at them, six or seven barking bloodhounds, and the outline of Sheriff Lester Smallwoods.

"Y'all didn't really think you could get away from me, did you?" the sheriff said gleefully.

"I'm telling you," J.L. said. "You've got the wrong man."

"That's what they all say," the sheriff replied.

The sheriff turned to a deputy.

"Cuff 'em," he ordered.

Two deputies stepped forward with handcuffs. They heard a distant whirring sound and looked up. A helicopter, bearing a U.S. Parks Service insignia, was directly overhead, shining a bright searchlight on the group. For a moment, the helicopter hovered steadily over the scene and then the pilot, bullhorn in hand, stuck his head out of the window.

"Lester! Lester Smallwoods!" the pilot shouted into the bullhorn. "What are you doing on federal property?"

"This man is wanted for murder and armed robbery," he shouted back, pointing to J.L.

"You know you have no jurisdiction on federal property," the pilot shouted. "You were warned about this last year."

"Yeah, I know, but—" the sheriff replied meekly.

"No buts about it," the pilot shouted back. "You have no authority on federal property."

The sheriff didn't reply.

"Suspect, show yourself!" the pilot barked.

J.L. turned and faced upward toward the voice.

"Cowboy! Cowboy!" the pilot shouted happily.

J.L. put his hand up to shade his eyes from the searchlight and peered upward toward the pilot.

"Hello!" he said, waving meekly into the blinding light.

"Cowboy!" the pilot said. "It's me! It's Ralph! Remember me?"

"It's the guy from the digital philosopher's convention," Karina said, waving back at him.

"Lester, are you crazy?" the pilot shouted. "This man wouldn't hurt a flea."

"He's wanted for murder and armed robbery in Illinois."

There was a pause and then, "Cowboy, what's your full name?"

"Jerome LaFayette Crockett."

"Let me check the computer," the pilot replied.

They waited.

"What's your date of birth?" the pilot shouted.

"June 17, 1973," J.L. replied.

They waited again.

"Lester, you stupid fricking redneck," the pilot shouted through the bullhorn. "That J.L. Crockett was captured five days ago in Indiana. This man here is innocent."

"Well, the names were similar," the sheriff said meekly.

"Shut up," the pilot said. "These people are going with me."

"Wait!" the sheriff interjected. "They tore the window out of the county jail."

"Let me call my base commander and tell him you're in violation of FL-1604 again," the pilot said, ducking back inside the helicopter.

"No! No!" the sheriff shouted frantically. "Don't call your commander. We'll get the jail window fixed. No problem!"

The pilot stuck his head out of the helicopter again.

"What about the warrant?" he shouted into the bullhorn.

"It's here!" the sheriff said, pulling a paper from his shirt pocket.

"Tear it up!" the pilot ordered.

The sheriff looked at the warrant and then back at the pilot.

"You heard what I said," the pilot shouted. "Tear it up in little pieces."

The sheriff shrugged and then tore the warrant into small pieces and threw it on the ground.

"Okay," the pilot replied. "Now get the hell off of federal property!"

The sheriff, his deputies, the dogs, and the flashlights turned and melted back into the darkness of the Everglades.

"All right, cowboy," the pilot said. "I'm sending down the rescue hoists for you and the little lady. You still going to Miami?"

"Yep!" J.L. said.

Moments later, J.L. and Karina were safely inside the helicopter.

"Y'all hang on!" the pilot instructed. "We're going to Miami."

They were thrown sideways as the mighty chopper did a U-turn and swept upward into the early morning sky. Moments later, after a bit of wobbling, the helicopter's flight leveled out and the passengers were riding smoothly

"Boy, I'm glad you found us," J.L. said to the pilot.

"I didn't find you," Ralph replied. "This onboard heat-seeking computer equipment is what found you," he replied.

"Then I'm glad the computer found us," J.L. said. "Karma is alive and well."

Ralph turned his attention to piloting the helicopter while J.L. and Karina rode quietly.

Finally, she turned to him.

"Okay," she said. "I've finished my part of the deal. Now I want to say goodbye."

He looked at her, saying nothing. Tears were forming in his eyes.

"What's wrong?" she asked.

He shook his head and looked away. She reached over, took his arms, and, with one arm in each hand, stared straight into his eyes.

"Tell me what's wrong."

He looked sadly into her eyes for a long moment. "I can't get on that boat," he said finally.

"What?"

"I could never go off and leave a woman who did for me what you did. You have shown me you love me and are devoted to me in a way I could never have imagined. You risked your life and your reputation for me. No woman has ever done that."

"What do you mean?"

"I'm taking you up on your offer," he said.

She stared at him incredulously.

"Let's go back and build a life together at Rancho Escobar," he said. "We can put a roof on the barn, rebuild those fences, and fix up the house and have a home and a life together."

She couldn't believe what she was hearing.

"Where did all this come from?" she asked.

"I'm a hard-headed guy," he said. "Until I see something for real right in front of my eyes, I don't believe it. Talk is cheap. When I saw you riding that mare, I knew you were the real deal. There's no plastic, no prostheses, no adornment. You're just you. I finally realized that. Oh God, I love that so much. I'm so tired of the falseness in this world. I was wrong about you. I'm sorry."

"Why didn't you take me up on my offer back at the ranch?"

"Because I wasn't sure about us," he said.

"Are you sure now?"

"Yes," he said quickly. "I'm sure now. I want you by my side. I want to share the rest of my life with you."

"But I want to be married," she said.

"We'll get married."

"Are you serious?"

"Of course I'm serious."

She couldn't believe what she was hearing.

"Just one more thing."

"What's that?"

"I want a son," he said. "Another little human being that I can watch grow up to be a man and share my life with."

She could see that he was dead serious.

"Oh my God, J.L.," she said blissfully. "I would love that. More than anything else on this earth, I would love to be your wife and have your child."

Then she stopped. "What about the money to pay the taxes on the ranch?"

"I've got $12,000 in a retirement plan at Bradford Wholesale Cattle Company. We can use part of that to pay the taxes. Also, I can file the claim for the stolen truck. That should be another $5,000. Together, we will figure it out."

"Oh, J.L.," she said. "You've made me so happy."

"Come on," he said. "Let's get started."

He turned to her and looked softly into her eyes.

"I love you," he said.

"I love you too," she said happily.

With that, he took her into his arms and kissed her.

J.L. broke the kiss when Ralph spoke up behind him.

"Okay, cowboy," Ralph said. "We're in Miami. Hang on!

We're going down."

"Ralph," J.L. called out over the whirring of the helicopter engine.

The pilot lowered the volume on his helmet radio and turned back to listen.

"Ralph, I'm sorry," J.L. said sheepishly. "I've changed my mind."

"Changed your mind?" Ralph asked, looking at J.L. curiously.

"Can you take us back to Port Everglades?"

"Port Everglades?" the pilot asked. "I thought you were going to Miami."

"Not anymore," J.L. replied. "I'm staying in the good old USA with the woman I love."

"You're sure now?"

"I'm sure."

"Absolutely sure?" Ralph asked again.

"Absolutely sure!" J.L. said confidently.

Ralph laughed happily. "Cowboy, you are one funny guy," he said. "Okay, Port Everglades it is."

Thirty minutes later, at first light of a new day, the U.S. Parks Service helicopter landed in the pasture at Rancho Escobar. J.L., holding his suitcase in one hand and Karina's hand in the other, waved goodbye to Ralph as the mighty chopper lifted back into the morning skies and headed back toward Miami.

Wedding

That night, J.L. turned himself loose with Karina. All the passion he had been holding inside he let run free and wild. *No holds barred tonight,* he told himself. *I have a direction in my life now. I'm in tune with my karma again.* Four separate times they joined their bodies together in physical union. It was a night both of them would always remember.

The next morning, they went into town to talk to the lawyer. Juan Ruiz was an overweight, balding man in his late forties with a thick mustache and ill-fitting clothes.

"Your aunt was very specific in her will," he began. "Since she had no children of her own, you were her favorite and she felt you were the one to inherit Rancho Escobar."

"What about the other heirs?" J.L. asked. "Her sisters and her mother."

"Her mother renounced all claims to the property," Juan said. "She said she was too old to rebuild it and wanted no part of it. The older sisters said they didn't have the money for the taxes and waived their claims."

"What about the younger sister Luz?" J.L. asked.

"We never could locate her."

"That's par for the course," Karina said.

Juan continued.

"There is $8,400 in outstanding taxes. If you pay half that amount and claim homestead exemption, the state will forgive the remainder."

"So $4200 will clear up the prior taxes?

The lawyer nodded.

J.L. and Karina looked at one another and smiled.

"We can pay that within a week," J.L. said.

"Then all you need to do is sign the papers," Juan said. "I'll give you all the info you need to pay the taxes."

Late that afternoon, J.L. opened an account at the single bank in Port Everglades and had $8,000 wired into it.

"Okay," he said, looking at the receipt, "This will get us started."

***

That afternoon, J.L. wrote a letter to Curly saying that he didn't end up in Argentina after all and was going to settle in Florida. He listed all of the books he wanted Curly to send and asked if he would be the best man at his wedding. In a return letter, Curly said he would send the requested books and announced he would be honored to be J.L.'s best man. Also, he said would talk to Will about coming to the wedding.

Two weeks later, on a clear, sunny day, J.L. and Karina were married in a small ceremony under the big cypress tree where J.L. had swung her in the childhood swing. Karina's mother and two of her sisters, Silvia and Ivette, served as bridesmaids. Curly, who flew in from Montana, served as best man. Other attendees included Will, Ralph, his wife, and their eleven-year-old daughter Angela, who served as ring-bearer.

The bride was radiant in white velvet and taffeta and J.L., wearing a tight-fitting suit he had found in a closet at Rancho Escobar, promised to love and honor his betrothed for all eternity. At the reception, Ralph announced he was going into politics. He said he planned to run for state senator in the upcoming election, but ultimately, he was setting his sights on becoming a U.S. Congressman. All of the qualified attendees promised Ralph their votes.

J.L. was as happy to see Curly and Will as they were to see him. When J.L. announced he was going to rebuild Rancho Escobar, they agreed to stay on for a while and help. Curly said his wife was visiting her sick mother in Arizona and Will explained he was in no hurry to get back to his part-time job working for a cattle auction company.

Following the reception, Mr. and Mrs. Crockett performed the dance of life for the attendees. It was a dance that spoke of life, of love, and the future. They were so incredibly happy.

Reflections II

Well, there you have it. All of that happened ten years ago. Since then, Karina and I have built a pretty good life for ourselves. I have to tell you Will and Curly were a big help rebuilding the ranch. The three of us, over a period of almost a month, rebuilt the barn, re-fenced and reseeded the back pasture, and did quite a bit of work on the house. After they left, it took me and Karina almost a year to get Rancho Escobar up and running as a true working ranch. We started with twelve head of cattle and four calves. After two years, we had more than sixty head. By 2012, our fourth year, we had just over 200 head. Today, thanks to the deal with the city, we have over a thousand head of cattle and almost 700 acres.

In 2013, the City of Port Everglades offered to buy Rancho Escobar. They said it was the last surviving old-style Spanish Rancho in Everglades County and they wanted to remodel it and make it into a tourist attraction. After Karina and I discussed it, she said any deal to buy the property would have to include a stipulation that we receive a percentage of the tourist revenue. After some hemming and hawing between the city council and our lawyer, they finally agreed and we struck a deal. It helped our finances a whole heap.

As luck would have it, just two weeks after the deal with the city, the property next door, which included 650 acres of fenced land, went up for sale. Using the money from the Rancho Escobar sale, we bought the land and built the Rocking K. As you might imagine, I named it after my wife.

Will's prediction that I would be the last cowboy hasn't come true yet. If fact, it may never come true now. Just last week, I talked to Ralph. He's a U.S. Congressman now and he has introduced a bill in Congress to outlaw electronic ranching. Ralph said such methods of cattle ranching are not only inhumane, but recent studies have shown that electronically raised cattle not only have tougher meat, but are more prone to disease. Ralph's bill has passed the house and is waiting for a vote in the senate. We'll wait and see what happens.

In 2008, a year after we were hitched up, Karina bore me a son, Joshua. There is no way to tell you how happy I was when I held that child in my arms the first time. Over the past ten years, he has become the light of my life. When a man has a child with a woman, it binds him to her in a way he could never be bound to a woman who has not had his child. It strengthened our love tenfold. From the day he was born, I had all these visions of teaching him to rope and ride and cut cattle, but he had no interest in those things. All he's interested in is computers and cell phones and video games and going on social media to talk to his friends.

Now, as I look across the pasture, I see him getting off the school bus. As the bus pulls away, he and Karina, with a handful of mail, are walking back toward the house. He's nine now and he's into anything and everything. Now he looks up and sees me on the porch and he's running like the wind to the house ahead of his mother. Here he comes.

"Daddy!!" the child said. "I got something to show you."

"What you got?"

Instantly, the child excitedly swung off his backpack, rifled through its contents, and withdrew a crumpled piece of paper. Proudly, he presented it to his father.

"I made an A in my science project," he said. "Can you believe that? My teacher said it was one of the best projects she had ever seen."

J.L. looked at the proffered paper.

"That's great!" the father replied, suddenly noticing the CD the child had in his hand. "What's that you've got?"

"*That's Invaders from Galaxy Molthar,* the new video game Tommy Jenkins let me borrow," Josh said. "After I change clothes, I'm going to Billy's house to play it with him. Mom said it was okay."

The child looked back suspiciously toward his mother, who was still reading mail as she slowly walked down the road to the house.

"I got something else," the child said, his voice going to a whisper.

"What?" J.L. whispered back.

The child reached into the backpack and withdrew a glass jar with a small snake inside.

"It's a garter snake," the child said. "I caught him at recess today. You can't tell Mama; she'll freak out. I'm going to keep him in my room."

J.L. smiled.

"What are you going to feed him?"

"Bugs," the child said. "Jimmy Adams has had one for almost a year. They're lots of fun and they scare girls to death."

The child checked his mother's status again. She was nearing the porch, still reading the mail.

"Okay," the child said. "I got to get ready to go to Billy's house... Now you won't tell Mama, will you?"

"Oh, no!" J.L. said. "It's a secret just between us."

"Promise?"

"Promise!" J.L. replied.

The child raised his hand for a high five. J.L. returned the gesture.

"Thanks, Dad!" the child said. "I gotta go now. Billy's dad will be here in a little while."

Instantly, the child returned the science paper and the snake to the backpack and, just as quickly as he arrived, disappeared into the house.

Moments later, Karina mounted the front porch and took a seat beside her husband on the porch swing.

"The water bill this month is almost $200. Where is all that water going?"

"It's been dry this spring," he said. "The cattle need extra water."

They sat quietly for several minutes, gently rocking in the swing. Finally, Karina spoke.

"Remember the time in South Georgia I got sick and you carried me in the rain...?"

J.L. looked at her wistfully.

"And the old black woman nursed you back to health...?" he said.

'Yeah," she said. "Her name was Selma."

"What made you think of that?"

"I don't know," she replied. "I'm just kind of weepy today."

They sat quietly, then looked up to see a late model sedan coming down the lane toward the ranch house.

"That's Josh's friend," J.L. said.

Seconds later, their son burst out of the house. He was carrying several video game CDs in his hand.

"What time you be back?" Karina asked.

"Eight o' clock," the child replied, testing the water.

"Let's make it seven," Karina replied. "You've got homework to do and you have to go to school tomorrow."

"Can we make it seven thirty?" the child ventured.

"Okay. Seven thirty," Karina said. "But not a minute later."

"Okay," the child said. "I'll be here at seven thirty. I'm gone. I love y'all."

The child quickly pecked his mother on the cheek.

"Bye!" Karina said. "Love you too."

"Bye!" the child said to his father. "Love you!"

"Love you too," J.L. said.

They watched as Josh bounded off the porch, got into the late model sedan and it started back down the lane. Moments later, the car disappeared down the main highway.

All was quiet again.

"You know he'll be gone in ten or twelve years," Karina said.

"What do you mean?"

"He'll be grown and married and gone," she replied. "And we'll be alone again."

"What are you getting at?"

"We won't be alone if we had another child," she said. "We'd have some company for another twenty years."

She put her hand on his knee.

"Do you want to have another child?" she continued. "The doctor said I could have another healthy child."

He looked at her and smiled.

"When do you want to get started?"

"There is no time like the present," she replied.

Then she hesitated.

"Can we eat first?" she asked. "Did you turn off the roast?"

"I did."

"Come on," she said. "Let's go eat."

J.L. stood up and placed his hat on his head. Then, with his boots in one hand and Karina's in the other, she opened the door and they went inside.

***

Tonight I'll bathe in her body like I do most nights. Only thing different tonight is we'll start shooting to have another child. Personally, I'd like another boy. I'd love to have another try at teaching a son to rope and ride and cut cattle, but I'm not sure if it will ever happen. Karina wants a girl. She says I had my shot and now it's her turn. She says she wants to have a daughter to teach all the things she had learned as a girl. Making dolls, teaching her cooking and sewing, and how to be a lady. I hope it doesn't take as long for her to get pregnant as it did last time. Last time, it took four months. She's thirty-seven now, but she shouldn't have any problem growing and delivering another child. She's healthy as a horse and has good strong periods every month. I'm not worried about it. We'll get it done. We always do. We make a good team.

The End

Other books by John Isaac Jones

A Quiet Madness: A biographical novel of Edgar Allan Poe

The Bird of Time

Alabama Stories

The Hand of God

The Duck Springs Affair

Thanks, PG!: Memoirs of a Tabloid Reporter

The Angel Years

For Love of Daniel

Thirteen Stories

Tembo Makaburi

Going Home

Lonely Magnolia

CPSIA information can be obtained
at www.ICGtesting.com
Printed in the USA
BVHW031152200622
640190BV00012B/245